Selena's Keepsake
By Linda Siebold

Book 2

Published by Forget Me Not Romances, an imprint of Winged Publications

Copyright © 2019 by Linda Siebold

ISBN-13: 9781794599291

Prologue

His long fingers shook as he pulled piece by piece from the dust and sorted the scraps of oak, walnut, pine, and bits of cherry on the workbench, wiping each with the soft rag. He drew out the measuring tape and marked a rectangle of pine for the base and four strips of walnut and oak for the short sides. He had enough oak for the two long sides, but the cherry was only enough for the top, so he set it aside.

After the pieces were cut, he smoothed them with sandpaper until they whispered *enough* and slid across his palm. *The last sanding makes it right. I don't want any splinters while working the pieces.* He set them in the correct order so he could place them on the base. The scent of the wood brought back so many memories. *Grandfather, do I have this right? Your puzzle boxes sold well from your little shop. Mother scolded me for bothering you, but you always had time for my eight-year-old self after Daddy left.*

Alternating the strips of oak and walnut for the short sides, he lined the first four strips on their edge with wood glue and clamped them together, then two pieces for the second side, saving the last two.

No, this looks wrong. Exhaling a deep breath, he stared at them, squeezing his eyes together in

1

concentration. *Why can't I see what's wrong? I want to remember how to build the puzzle box before my mind chooses not to...*

He clenched his fingers until arthritic knuckles began to ache. *The lip. The top strip is a lip.* After undoing the clamps, he shifted the top piece on each side so the top strip made a right angle. When they were dry, he drilled holes for the brass pins and glued the box.

He perched onto the old stool and started on the intricate top. First he pieced...fit, then added...back. When all was ready, he glued.

With hands raised to the light, he studied his palms, noticing the lines and callouses. *Your hands were scarred and rough too, Grandfather. I remember watching you setting the pieces in the candlelight. Hands that were so gentle, but strong. You were gone before I knew it. Would you approve of the man I became? Have I done my best like you told me to when I sat beside your bench? I'll see you again...*

When the inside rails were dry and he set the lid, the box was ready.

Chapter One

*D*ear Journal, it's Selena. I haven't written for a while. A lot of things have happened since I wrote last. I love my new office as I'm in my own space now. R & S Retrievals bought the storefront next door and remodeled it just for me. It was messy when they cut the hole in the brick wall between the buildings, but now it's done and I've moved in, shelves, filing cabinets, and all.

The two agents of R& S Retrievals have become three now as Sam and Matt brought in a new partner. Michael Rickard, a former FBI agent. His dry sense of humor keeps us on our toes. Of course I have to look up to him since he's about a foot taller than me.

Sam and Matt have been out of the office a lot delivering the Carmichaels' stolen goods back to their rightful owners. More stashes will keep them occupied for quite a while. The ruby necklace, the contessa's, is in its vault in Montaire's museum.

My research work has been non-stop. It's been challenging but satisfying. In the last few months, I've worked on cases from the local and state cop shops and even as far away as Scotland Yard. Montaire is running smoothly as far as I can tell from reports.

Sam and I spend as much time together as we can.

He still hasn't asked me the big question yet, but I'm hoping it's soon. Maybe he'll catch marriage fever when we go to Kim's wedding this weekend at Palm Keys.

Haylie and I are flying down early in the morning, so I'd better quit and finish my packing.

~

As Selena Simmons and Haylie Stevens dragged their luggage from the Orlando terminal down the broad aisle, a stray feeling of danger furrowed Selena's brows and made her uneasy. She glanced at the faces in the busy airport. Families jostled for position in the hotel shuttle lines. Business travelers with overnight cases strode by on their cell phones. Tour groups gathered together, waiting for buses to pick them up. *Maybe I'm just getting paranoid. Why would someone be threatening two friends coming for a wedding? No danger here. Still, someone is watching us.* She gripped the handle of her bag.

"Do you think the guys are missing us yet?" Haylie asked.

"Maybe," Selena grinned at her friend.

Sam Russell, the tall dark-haired man of Selena's dreams, had driven Selena and Haylie to the airport, and Matt Stevens, his partner in R & S Retrievals and Haylie's husband, was delivering jewelry, more stolen pieces from another of the Carmichaels' stashes, to a family in Kansas City. He would fly down at the end of the week for the ceremony and events to follow. The new agent, Michael Rickard, and Dex, Sam's German shepherd, manned the office in their absence.

"Maybe," Selena grinned at her friend.

They followed the signs pointed toward the rental car section and turned down the ramp.

As the crowd thinned, Selena stopped. Haylie glanced at her. "Everything okay?"

A shiver darted down Selena's back as shoes

scuffled behind them on the concrete walkway. Her fingertips guided Haylie to the side with their backs against the wall. Danger nagged, and she wanted to face it head-on. A dark-haired man in a business suit smiled at them as he passed by.

No sense in borrowing trouble. Maybe Sam was right when he insisted I take a little down time from the responsibilities of being Contessa Selena for a while. Maybe it was the combination of work and those responsibilities. She'd just had the heebie-jeebies since the plane took off this morning. Maybe it was merely her imagination that someone was following them. She said, "I just wanted to make sure I had the name of the car agency before we got there."

~

The man smiled in satisfaction as he noted the women drive away in the bright red Lamborghini from where he stood in the shadows. She was here. Now to start the process.

~

Selena leafed through the brochures on Palm Keys as Haylie finessed the five-speed Lamborghini, weaving through rush-hour traffic. Kim Essex, one of Haylie's college roommates, and Tommy Masters, her fiancé, were to be married in a private resort on Florida's east coast. The gazebo off the manicured grounds that looked over the ocean was the essence of romance. This was the first time Selena had attended a destination wedding. She could imagine the sea breezes now, ruffling her hair, as they watched the ceremony.

A husky bass voice from the GPS system directed their way.

"I think I need to change the voice on my Porsche to one that sounds like this. Matt would hate it. But, I'll give him a break and leave it like it is until he does something stupid again like let Sam drive my baby."

Hayley wrinkled up her nose.

Selena laughed. "That would do it. Sam takes driving seriously especially if a bad guy is involved. No idea is too dangerous then, and semis are a lot bigger when they get really close."

The man's voice said, "In two miles exit Highway 95 North."

"We're almost there. I can smell the beach. Can you?" Haylie sniffed.

"Exit left to Highway 95 North." The voice directed again. "In ten miles the resort is on your right."

Both grinned when they drove through the gates to the resort.

Selena said, "It's pretty frilly."

The resort property, dotted with tropical flowers, was green and luxurious. The main building covered acres of ground and its façade was adorned with curlicues and vine-covered trellises. Angel figurines peeked through the landscaping.

Haylie giggled. "Looks like Barbie run amok."

"It should be pink," Selena said. "I can't wait for the guys' reactions."

They pulled under the portico, and a valet rushed out for the keys, the porter following in his wake for the luggage.

Selena and Haylie stepped from the revolving door into a large registration area with busy desks on both sides. Massive pillars dotted the room, holding up a lofty ceiling frescoed with more angels. Ivory stucco walls circled the room. Panels of veined mirrors with gold frames lined the long desk's back counters. Small palm trees in golden planters added a tropical feel.

"I don't think we're in Kansas anymore," Haylie quipped, and her eyes twinkled.

Selena grinned.

After settling into their queen-size room, Haylie

suggested exploring the hotel.

They reached the mezzanine. "That's crazy. This place is covered by one roof and even has a canal running through it. Look at the people riding on the boat." Selena leaned over the rail on a walkway. "I can't believe all the shops on that level. There are so many rooms and suites above us. With the restaurants and shops here, it's almost like a city. Look up at the glass roof."

Haylie unfolded the map. "This area is listed as the Everglades District. Our room's in the Continental. There's even a water park on the south side of the complex. Guess what it's called? The Blue Lagoon. That's where all the families would be. Surely we can miss walking over there."

Selena nodded. "I think I'm about ready to grab some early supper and call it a night. That restaurant over there with steak and seafood would be the logical place for a salad."

The hostess seated them in a booth a little way from the bar.

"Tell me about the other bridesmaids," Selena requested.

"There are four. You've met Amelia Masters. She's Tommy's sister and a sweetheart."

"Is she the brunette who came with Kim the last time she visited?"

Haylie nodded. "Katie Perkins is a high school softball coach in Missouri someplace. She makes you laugh when you're around her. She was always busy with sports when we were in school, but Kim, Katie, and I hung out when we could."

The waitress introduced herself and took their order.

"Jocelyn Jones is the fourth. She was the party girl of the bunch. Pretty and popular in the wrong kind of way. She's drop-dead gorgeous on the outside, but not so much on the inside. Jocelyn roomed with us the last year. She thought Matt was fair game."

Selena rolled her eyes. "She's the one you think might try to ruin the wedding?"

"Not if I can help it." Haylie's eyes flashed. "She might try but—"

"Ladies," the waitress approached the booth. "The two gentlemen at the bar would like to buy you a drink, if you'd like."

"Why is it that guys think you're fair game when you're out with another woman?" Haylie grumbled and raised her left hand so the stone in her wedding ring glittered in the light.

Selena grinned at Haylie and the waitress. "Please thank them, but tell them definitely 'no.' We're not interested."

"Now if you'd been Jocelyn, she'd flutter her eyelashes and motion them over."

"You don't like her too much, do you?"

"Nope."

Selena laughed. *Tomorrow and these next few days should be interesting.*

When they opened the door to their room, Haylie's cell phone rang. She sat down on the bed, pulled her shoes off, and propped the pillows against the headboard to lie against. "I was hoping you would call. I've been missing you... Did you get the necklace and earrings back to the owners okay? Oh, she did. I bet that made you feel good to give them to her. I would have cried right along with her... Selena's fine. We got to the resort about four, I guess. You ought to see the vehicle we're driving...No, not a Rolls. A Lamborghini, and it's bright red...Don't worry. I like my baby better..."

Selena nabbed her pajamas out of her suitcase and slipped into the bathroom to get ready for bed. When she came back out, she said, "All yours."

Haylie was already sound asleep.

She plugged in her phone, and as her fingers twisted the switch and turned off the light, her phone rang. "Hello."

"How's my girl?" Sam's voice caressed her through the distance.

Selena snuggled under the sheet and lay in the darkness, waiting for her heart rate to slow to normal. "How's my Sam?"

"Missing you. Did you have a good flight?"

"Smooth. I didn't know Haylie was scared to fly."

"She never has been. She's usually guessing the RPMs of the plane," Sam chuckled. "What makes you think that?"

"As soon as she got on the plane, she was white knuckling the seat belt in the cabin."

Sam hemmed. "That doesn't sound like her. Matt said she's been a little quiet the last couple of weeks, not feeling well and more tired than usual."

"I'll make her slow down while we're here. She slept most of the way here. Maybe she's just tired. Is everything there okay?"

Sam asked, "Why do you ask?"

Leave it to Sam to be suspicious. "No reason. I just wanted to make sure everybody was okay." Selena said.

"We're pretty quiet right now with just some little cases ongoing. Nothing's new at Montaire, according to Toby when I talked to him last. No work. You're supposed to take a break this week." He scolded.

"Okay. I know I promised," Selena smiled. *That doesn't mean the feeling's not there. What is it?*

"I've got some news about Miss Essie. You know how I've tried talking her into going into assisted living? One of her friends from church recently moved into the new complex down the road from the cabin. The apartment next to hers was available, so Miss Essie

9

signed the lease this afternoon."

"What?"

"Uh, huh. That's what I thought. What clinched it was Dex was welcome to visit her anytime, and we, meaning me, can transplant some of her flowers outside her window. Moving day is tomorrow. Matt and I jumped at the opportunity in case she changed her mind. She'll give us her marching orders around eight, and we'll move what she wants to take with her, and the rest will go into my storage area at the cabin."

"The rest of the old folks will like the dog for sure. There will be all kinds of treat jars set out. He'll roll down the halls." A yawn escaped Selena's lips. "Sorry, Sam. You're not boring. I'm getting sleepy."

"I bet you're tired. Dex and I wanted to say goodnight. I'll call back tomorrow around the same time. Have fun. I'll see you Thursday evening. I love you, Selena."

"I love you, too. Give Dex a hug for me." *I miss you too*. The call clicked off, and she set the phone back on the lampstand. Her arms ached for him as she gazed at the detection lights blinking on the ceiling. Danger lurked as her eyes shuttered closed.

Chapter Two

The next morning Haylie ended her call and smiled at Selena. "Kim and her family are here. It sounds like we have until two to get to the dress fitting. She said there's a large outdoor market near the shop. Do you want to check it out?"

Zipping in and out of traffic in the sleek Lamborghini, the ride to the market was quick. They parked near the dress shop and entered the market, strolling through the booths.

"I like the bright pottery." Haylie pointed to a turquoise plate in a potter's booth. "That would look nice on my new shelf." She picked it up and set it back down gently as she pointed at a chip on the back.

Selena stopped by a booth with woven suncatchers. She flipped the price tag over and passed on by.

A vendor called out to them, "I have some keepsakes for you, pretty ladies. Stop inside. All are handcrafted. I make them in my shop."

Selena and Haylie weaved through his area of wooden items. Large furniture lined the back, and tables displaying boxes and chests filled the rest of the space. A small box caught Selena's attention. "Look, Haylie. This little box reminds me of Gran's chest I've told you about. It has little animals inlaid on it." She picked it up, rubbed its shiny surface with her fingertips, and a piece of wood slid to the side.

"It's a puzzle box," Haylie grinned at the surprise on Selena's face. "You didn't break it. My uncle is a woodworker and likes to make them." She checked her watch. "We'd better go and meet the others."

Selena crossed to the vendor. "How much are you asking for this box?"

The vendor was quiet for a beat. "Twenty-five dollars, miss."

Strange. It's almost as if it wasn't his to sell or he couldn't decide how much to ask. "I'd like it, please."

~

Selena tucked the puzzle box inside her tote as Kim, her mom, Kathy, and the other bridesmaids waited at the door. She hugged Kim and her mom and grinned at Amelia. Katie's brown eyes twinkled. *She's going to make things lively.* Jocelyn cocked her head and looked at Selena with pursed lips. *I can tell who's who simply by looking.*

The group found seats on a sectional by the dressing rooms. Selena sat between Haylie and Kathy.

"Miss Jones requested that each of you try your dresses on one at a time so she can make any adjustments." Kathy said. "She'll find shoes for us after the fittings."

"I'll go first." Amelia volunteered and headed for the dressing room. "I can't wait to see my dress."

"Kim wanted all the bridesmaids to wear the same color of dress, but in a style they liked." Kathy glanced at Selena.

The women chattered until Amelia came back out.

"Wow, that color looks nice on you." Kim nodded. "I like the style you've chosen, the A-line with the sparkle at the round neck and down both sides of the bodice."

12

"I like the pleats on the skirt. It's full, but not ball-gown full. Fun to be able to move around in." Amelia twirled in front of the mirror.

"It's kind of plain, isn't it?" Jocelyn muttered.

"It's not plain. It's flattering, Amelia." Haylie narrowed her eyes at Jocelyn.

Selena smiled at Amelia. "I love it." The uncertainty caused by Jocelyn's comment lifted a little.

Miss Jones nodded. "It fits well."

"I'm next," Katie popped up to follow Amelia to the dressing room.

"See what I mean?" Haylie cocked her head and whispered to Selena.

Katie strode back in with her dress. Hers was a simple off-the-shoulder style that draped around her toned shoulders, highlighting her lithe figure.

"You look amazing, Katie." Kathy smiled.

"That's fine," Miss Jones said.

"Not bad for a jock," Jocelyn muttered.

Katie stopped and assumed a muscle pose in response.

"My turn," Haylie sprang up before Jocelyn could rise to her feet. She returned a few minutes later in a halter-style dress with an open back.

"I love it, Haylie. That looks awesome on you. The drape on the skirt adds extra drama." Kim hugged her. "My matron of honor will outshine me."

Haylie laughed. "Very doubtful. I love your dress. You'll look like a princess and make Tommy faint."

"I guess I'll be okay as Katie knows CPR," Kim quipped. "I'm hoping to dazzle him when he sees me."

"It fits the best of them all so far," Miss Jones announced. "It's lovely on you."

Jocelyn huffed and pushed off the couch.

With her hands clenched, Haylie stood where she was, and Jocelyn brushed past her into the dressing area.

"My, she's unpleasant, Kim. I'm sorry I encouraged you to invite her." Kathy Essex sighed.

Kim shrugged. "Don't worry, Mom. It's okay. If she goes overboard, I can uninvite her. I'll sic Tommy and his brothers on her."

"I think you can draft Sam and Matt if you need them too. Matt's not too fond of her either." Haylie chuckled.

Minutes passed. Jocelyn hadn't come out of the dressing room.

Katie grinned. "The slow poke gives me time to tell my latest story. One of my softball girls 'missed' the bus home from our games in Scranton last week. She made a couple of errors on our last game, so she ran out to the bus before the rest of the girls, piled her stuff in the back seat like she was pouting in the corner, and scrambled off the bus before we got back. It looked authentic, and she's a drama queen anyway. Her buddy, Judy, got on and sat beside her stuff with body language screaming something was off."

"Don't tell me she had it planned?" Haylie asked.

"Oh, yeah. She was going to ride home with her boyfriend, who happens to be the school superintendent's son, and it was my fault I left her. Judy was part of the plan. When the rest of the girls were on the bus and only a few cars were left around us, I instigated a roll call just to make her answer. I called the girls name by name. With each name Judy started to fidget. When I called 'Meredith' twice and she didn't answer, the other girls sensed by then that something was afoot. I got up and headed slowly to the back of the bus, peering side to side. With each step I took, Judy's face got whiter and whiter."

"I'll go check the young lady to make sure she doesn't need assistance," Miss Jones glanced at her wristwatch. "Jenny, my assistant, was back there earlier."

Kim nodded. "Go on, Katie."

"Anyway, I got back there and Judy's eyes got huge when I poked Meredith's stuff in the corner. I got eyeball-to eyeball with Judy and asked, 'Where is she?'

"Judy, now in tears, said, 'She's riding home with Justin.'

"I pulled my cellphone out of my pocket to dial Mr. French, the superintendent, as I'd seen him at the game earlier, but lo and behold, I turned and Mr. French stood outside the door with his son and Meredith in tow. Seems like Mr. French had driven up with Justin that day, and Meredith slid into the seat beside him…"

"Whoops," Haylie giggled. "Give me kindergartners any day."

Voices came from the fitting room. You will not represent my shop with that dress. I cannot let that out enough to make it decent." Miss Jones, her red face contorted in anger and hands balled into fists, followed Jocelyn from the dressing room.

"I think it looks nice, "Jocelyn climbed up on the step and swiveled around to admire herself in the three-way mirror. The low-cut dress barely contained her bust, and the short hem looked like a long shirt.

Katie snorted. "Not too flattering, Jocelyn."

"Why? Because I don't look like a man in it?"

Haylie's eyes flashed, and she took a step toward Jocelyn.

Selena jumped to her feet and slipped in the middle. *Oh, no. Jocelyn, you're not going to ruin things for Kim and that poor lady. And, I'm not going to explain to Matt how I had to bail Haylie out on assault charges.* "Haylie, do you remember that dress that Madame Resa had in her shop in Montaire? It was slim-fitting with the draped, cowl neck. When I tried it on, I loved it, but Madame Resa said a coronation gown had to be full."

15

Haylie narrowed her eyes at Selena and slowly unclenched her fists. The fire in her eyes cooled a little. "Yes. It was deceptive. The gown fit like butter and hugged in all the right places."

"Coronation?" Jocelyn stuttered.

"I am Contessa Selena Carmichael-Simmons from Montaire. You may have seen pictures of the ceremony. It was on the news."

"I—uh—may have."

Selena walked over to Mrs. Jones. "I believe you have a dress similar to the one I was talking about. I saw it hanging near the wedding dresses as we came in. It was in a royal blue color, if I remember. Hopefully you have one in the flamingo pink like the rest? Would you please let Jocelyn try it on?"

Mrs. Jones took a deep breath. "Yes, of course. I believe that would look nice on her. Come on, dear. Let's try that one on."

Jocelyn followed Mrs. Jones without a word.

"Thanks, Selena," Haylie said. "I was ready to smack her."

Katie put her hands on her hips and sauntered over to Haylie. "I'd have helped, dahling."

"I like your Mae West impersonation, Katie," Kim chuckled. "I remember when we went to the costume party and you wore the blond wig and high heels."

"Yeah. I remember. I fell off the darn heels and sprained my ankle. Coach was mad because I was out for a week."

Selena laughed. "I wish I would've had you three for roommates when I was in school. Mine were boring and studied all the time."

"That's okay. We'll adopt you."

Jocelyn glided back out of the dressing room with Miss Jones at her heels.

"Oh, that's lovely," Selena circled Jocelyn and

nodded to Miss Jones.

"It's very attractive, "Miss Jones agreed and let out a relieved breath.

"I think Kim said something about shoes to match. I'm thinking strappy sandals with lower heels would be the perfect thing for a wedding on the beach. Is that what you prefer, Kim?" Selena asked.

"Yes."

"Good. What's next on the agenda?"

Kathy sighed. 'Crisis averted' relief crossed her face. "The salon expects us at 4:00 for manicures and pedicures."

Chapter Three

Michael Rickard ran his long fingers through Dex's shiny coat. "Just you and me, Dex. I'm glad it's me who's manning the office. We'll leave the moving to Sam and Matt. If it stays quiet, we'll go out in a bit for a cheeseburger. Does that sound good to you?"

Dex eyed him and wagged his tail from his place in the spot of sunshine emanating through the window. He tilted his head toward the main office door as the alarm for the front door buzzed.

"Busted. We must have a customer. No cheeseburgers right now." Michael pushed back his chair and strode to the reception area where a tall, slender woman about his age waited. She whirled around and faced him, her honey-colored skin, green eyes, and a punch of her beauty walloped him. He managed to say, "Hello," then his voice dried up.

"Is this R & S Retrieval Agency?"

"Yes."

"I'm a friend of Haylie Stevens. I teach fourth grade at the same school where she teaches."

"And your name is...I'm Michael Rickard," he stuttered.

"My name is Angel Townsend. Haylie has

encouraged me to come see her husband or Sam Russell. I need help finding my daughter, Laura. My ex-husband has taken her and I don't know where she is. The police refuse to look for her since his lawyer has drawn up papers saying I'm an unfit mother. I'm not."

Michael's heart shattered a little to see the tears glisten in her eyes.

"I'm afraid for my daughter. My ex-husband works for some unscrupulous people. He's violent, travels a lot, and people end up missing or dead after he leaves. We've been divorced since Laura was three months old, and he hasn't been interested in her at all since that time until six months ago when he filed for joint custody."

"That must be tough for you."

"A judge fell for his lies and granted every other weekend visitation. A month ago Ethan picked her up for the weekend and didn't bring her home. His lawyer filed papers and supposed proof against me with the same judge who granted visitation. He ruled that Ethan had full custody without a hearing. My court-appointed lawyer said he couldn't do anything, that the papers were in order. I can only pay so much right now." She held out a hundred-dollar bill.

"Why don't you come into my office. We'll worry about the fees later."

The woman named Angel followed and perched at the end of one of his guest chairs. She folded the money and stuck it back into her purse with a sigh. Dex walked over to her so she could run his hands on his fur.

"We can look into it, Miss Townsend. I need some more information. Your ex-husband's name, birthday, and local address?" Michael removed a legal pad and pen out from his top drawer, angled it to the left, and scribbled as she answered.

"Ethan Wright, June 12, 1978, 512 Claymore. That wouldn't help you though because he cleaned everything out."

"Phone number?" Michael's eyes met hers.

Pain crossed her features. "Disconnected. It was 785-234-2279."

"We can check out calls before it was disconnected for a pattern. Maybe he went to a place he's been before. Do you have a photograph of your daughter and your ex?"

She leaned over and pulled out two pictures from her wallet. "This is Laura's school picture last fall." Her hand trembled as she smoothed a bent corner flat. "The only picture I have of Ethan is our wedding photo. I pulled it out of the album this morning." She slid them across the desk.

Michael noted the girl's photo. *She looks a lot like her mother. It's too bad the worry has taken away Angel's smile. He'd like to make her smile.* He brushed that thought aside and pulled the other photo over. He froze. The eyes of Ethan Murray smirked up at him. *Ethan Murray, the hired assassin who killed Jeremy and almost killed me in the FBI sting...*

"Are you all right, Mr. Rickard?" Angel asked.

"Yes. I'm fine. I knew your ex-husband when he used another name. He's on the FBI wanted list. A dangerous man. There won't be any fee to find your daughter except maybe for some expenses we can work out. How can I reach you?"

As soon as Angel walked out of the office, Michael texted Selena. "I just took a case. I was going to wait till next week, but it's one where a girl's life is involved. Ask Haylie if she knows Angel Townsend and find out what info she has. Her girl has been taken by a known hit man—the client's ex. He goes by Ethan Wright. I knew him as Ethan Murray. He's the one who shot my FBI partner. Let me know."

He googled as much information as he could on the

case, but it was slow going. Selena could have delved much deeper in minutes. His cell phone pinged.

Away from my laptop right now. I'll text you back later.

"Well, I guess I'll wait, Dex. Are you ready for a cheeseburger now? We can make it lunch/dinner. I'm hungry."

Dex stood, wagged his tail, and sniffed something on the floor by the door.

"What do you have there, buddy?" Michael leaned down and picked up the driver's license on the floor. "Whoops. She might need this. We'll drop it off on the way."

~

Dex's muzzle rested on the edge of the open window. He sprawled across the seat and watched as Michael stared at the house.

"Not too bad of a little bungalow, but it could use a little TLC though. Paint, shingles, new windows. Stay, Dex. I'll drop this off and we'll be on our way." Michael strode up the sidewalk and pressed the doorbell, alert for any sounds coming from the house, but it was quiet. He palmed the card in his hand and turned back to the car.

Dex was standing on the seat, leaning out the window.

Michael opened his door, and Dex whimpered. "What's wrong, buddy?"

Dex jumped out and ran toward the side of the house to an old privacy fence covered with bougainvillea.

"Darn it, Dex. Come back here." Michael chased him and peered over the fence to see an older man lying across the steps in the sun. Michael unlatched the gate, and Dex ran inside. The dog plopped down on his haunches beside the man and licked his hand.

Michael ran up to see the man's eyes open and his hand reach out to pet the dog. "Are you okay, sir?"

"Yes. I'm fine, just can't get up. I've got to get back into the house before I get into trouble. I wanted to check the bird feeder before Laura called."

Michael took a second look at the old man. He knew him. "Pops? Is that you?"

The old man grabbed his arm, and Michael helped him up. "Point guard. Rickard. The state team in 1993. You played with the Simms twins. You've got a friend with you."

"That's Dex. He knew you were out here. Yes, I'm Michael Rickard."

"Well, come in, Michael. Your friend can come in too. I need something to drink." Pops slid the patio door open, limped inside, and eased himself into a well-worn recliner. "Angel has some sweet tea made in the refrigerator. I'll take a glass. You can have one too."

Michael searched through the cupboards until he found the glasses. He filled them with ice, poured tea, and set them on the lampstand by Pops before sitting on a chair nearby.

"Thank you. What did you say your name was?"

"It's Michael. Are you sure you're not hurt, Pops?"

"There was a point guard named Michael when the team won state in 1993. He became a policeman, I think."

"That's me."

A car door slammed out front and a heavyset blond woman walked in. She pulled out a casserole from the refrigerator, slipped the lid off, and spooned some of the contents in the sink. Water splashed as her fingers flipped the garbage disposal switch on and off. Then she set a couple plates from the cupboard and some silverware in the drainer. She returned the casserole to the refrigerator. It was only then that she glanced into the living room to look for Pops.

Michael's mouth tightened as she glanced at the

glasses on the lampstand. He noted the surprise that crossed her face.

The garage door growled open, and Angel walked in. She crossed the floor to hug her father and covered the surprise at seeing Michael there. "Hi, Pops. How was your day?"

"One of my boys came to see me."

"I see that, Pops. It's Michael, isn't it?" Her lips curled up a little at the ends.

"Michael was the name of the point guard on the 1993 state team." He repeated.

"Thanks, Donna. I'm home for the evening. We'll see you in the morning." Angel called to the lady in the kitchen as she ambled to the door.

"Night, Pops."

Pops pushed the television remote and glanced at Angel. "Laura didn't call today. Is she coming home soon?"

"She'll be home soon, Pops. You go ahead and watch your show while I make supper."

He nodded. "Thanks for coming, Michael."

Michael followed Angel into the kitchen as Dex padded over and lay on the floor by Pops. "Dex and I found your dad on the ground in the backyard a little while ago. He wasn't hurt, but he couldn't get up. I don't know how long he'd been there."

Angel stared at him. Her eyes lost some sparkle. "Where was Donna?"

"Was that Donna? She walked in five minutes ago and dumped something from a casserole dish down the garbage disposal. My guess is she hasn't been around all day."

"Don't tell me that," she snapped. "The lady at SRS sent her to be a companion during the day. She's supposed to give him his noon meds and make his lunch. The doctor said the medicine would slow his dementia. I pay her well. What do you want? I gave you all the information I have to look for Laura and tried to give you what I could afford."

"Look, I'm just trying to help. I was one of Pop's boys. I care and don't want him hurt. Dex and I brought your driver's license back. You dropped it in the office." Michael's tawny brown eyes met her green ones. He lowered his voice and repeated, "I want to help."

"Is supper ready, Angel? I'm hungry."

"Just about, Pops. I'll bring you some casserole in a minute."

"I've got a couple of motion cameras I can set up, one in this main room and one on the back porch. I can watch them on my phone tomorrow to see if it's what I suspect. Dex and I can be here in minutes if things look funky while you're at school. Then, we'll check the recording out after you get home. Okay?"

She nodded.

"I've given your information to Selena, our information specialist. She was away from her laptop when I texted her. She'll run the information through her databases, and that'll give us a place to start to find your daughter."

Chapter Four

*L**aura Townsend, Angel Townsend, Ethan Wright,
Ethan Murray, contract killings of businessmen or
women and their dates within the last three
months.* Selena entered the last of the data Michael had
requested into her laptop and set the search into motion.
He sounded a little funny when he'd said the one name,
Murray. It triggered a memory of when Sam and Matt
were vetting Michael. She'd done his background check.
Murray was the name of the killer in Michael's last FBI
case. She picked up her cell phone and texted Sam. "The
missing child case Michael's working on may involve
his last FBI case. Love you."

She ran the puzzle box through her hands. Her
fingers rubbed the smooth finish as she rolled it around.
The wood seemed to warm with her touch.

"Are you about ready for breakfast?" Haylie slipped
on her shoes.

"Sounds good. Look, I've gotten a little further on
the box."

Haylie smiled. "You'll get it. Uncle Marvin's boxes
had a switch. When you get to a certain point, they
unlatch more than one slide. Then, presto, they open.
Maybe this one's the same."

Selena stuck the puzzle box in her tote, then grabbed

her laptop. "Michael's in a hurry for his information, so I'll take it along. By the way, do you know Angel Townsend?"

"Yes," Haylie admitted. "She's in the next block in my building, but I visit with her in the teacher's lounge every once in a while. Her ex-husband ran off with her daughter months ago. She's pretty sad all the time. I'm glad she finally came in."

"She's Michael's new missing-daughter case."

~

Michael checked his email as soon as he arrived at the office the next morning. Selena should have something for him soon. He pushed the app on his phone to check the cameras on Angel's and Pops' place and shifted it onto his screen. Angel, dressed in slacks and a pretty blouse, was at the stove making breakfast, and Pops leaned against the counter nearby talking to her. From her response yesterday, he didn't think she'd allow Pops to get hurt on purpose. She was protective. The caretaker was a different story. How could the caretaker leave him unattended like that? Yesterday was so scary; it was fairly cool out. But, today the temperature was supposed to be over a hundred degrees. At least he could be there in minutes if need be...

Pop moved over and sat at the table. Angel pulled two plates out of the cupboard and handed the silverware to Pops. He set them at their places while she dished out the bacon and scrambled eggs and then sat down. She handed him a glass of water and watched him take his pills. Then they prayed. A few minutes later she picked up the empty plates, took them to the sink, and poured Pops another cup of coffee. Pops watched her wash and dry the dishes and hung the towel on its rod. She glanced outside. *The caretaker must be there.* Angel walked behind Pops, threw her arms around his neck, and kissed him on the cheek. He pushed back his chair and ambled to his chair in the living room.

The caretaker sauntered into the kitchen and told Angel, "Good morning," and called to Pops. The light on the television flashed and a game show came on. Angel gathered her purse and briefcase and walked out the back door to the garage.

The caretaker set her purse down on the counter and watched out the window as Angel backed out and drove away. She waited a few seconds, slinked to the refrigerator, and pulled out ingredients for a sandwich. As she sat at the table and ate her sandwich, she kept glancing at her watch.

What are you up to, lady?

Pops had fallen asleep in his chair.

"What are you watching?" Sam strode into the office with Dex at his heels.

Michael grinned. "Remember the case I told you about yesterday? The one with the missing girl?"

Sam nodded.

"The lady dropped her driver's license on the floor when she was here. Dex found it, and we took it back to her house. Her dad lives there too, and he'd fallen in the backyard. He has the beginning stages of dementia or Alzheimer's, and she's hired a caretaker when she's gone during the day. But, he was alone. The caretaker wasn't there. I suspect she's collecting the money and leaving as soon as Angel leaves."

"Elder abuse?"

"Yes. The client's got her hands full. I talked to Selena about research on the case. She's running the search this morning. I called in some other favors from my old section boss too. The girl's dad has been on the FBI list for quite a while. He went by Murray then. The perp killed my partner and almost me in a sting. He got away then... This is the closest we've been for over three years."

Sam nodded. "Keep us posted. Matt and I are headed to the airport around noon. Thanks for letting Dex hang out with you. We've got all of Miss Essie's stuff taken care of. I told her to call you if she needs anything."

As soon as the outer door closed, Dex padded back to his spot of sunshine on the carpet, and Michael settled back to watch the screen.

The kitchen was empty. Pops was still asleep in his chair. *Where was the woman?*

Michael rewound the recording to where he'd left off when Sam came in. The woman finished her sandwich, threw away the trash, and cleaned up. She looked at her watch again and paced in front of the kitchen window. Light beamed off metal in the street and its glint shone in the window. The caretaker grabbed her purse and went out the door. *Gotcha.*

Michael worked on paperwork and glanced occasionally at the box from the camera feed he'd pulled down into the corner.

Pops woke up around eleven-thirty. He pushed out of his chair and lumbered into the kitchen. He pulled the casserole dish out of the refrigerator, set it on the counter, and lifted the lid. He wrinkled his nose and put it back.

You hungry, Pops? It's been a long time since breakfast. Michael glanced down at the dog. "Hey, Dex. You ready for your cheeseburger? We didn't get one yesterday, and it looks like Pops is hungry too."

Chapter Five

D ad, isn't that Mrs. Mills, the nice lady we met in Georgia?" Laura Townsend asked as a bulletin scrolled across the bottom of the television screen. "She's dead. Police are looking for her killer. They suspect a man traveling in a blue car…"

Her father rose from the desk and grabbed the remote out of her hand. "I told you no television. Do you remember what I told you I'd do with your mother and your grandfather if you didn't follow my directions?"

She cringed as her father stepped closer, his icy blue eyes spearing her. Now, she knew why he dragged her to places and followed certain people. And, she'd thought he just wanted her with him because he loved her. He didn't love her. He never did. He used her to get to that lady. He told her so that day in the park, "You get her to feel sorry for you since your mother died. Your mother's not dead, but I can change that."

She shook her head. Why didn't she listen to her mom when she'd said he might hurt her? She didn't want to believe it. He was her dad. She fought with her mom before he picked her up for that weekend, screaming at her because she wanted to go live with him. All the rest of the kids had dads or stepdads. Her mom didn't want her to be like the other kids. Now all she wanted was to go home to Mom and Pops.

Tears fell as she realized she didn't have anything left. Her puzzle box was gone. She'd left it on the table at the market and the red-haired lady bought it.

He killed Mrs. Mills and the others too. The constant moving around. It made sense now. He was a monster. He used her to get close to those people. The horror of it all made her stomach hurt. She held her breath as he drew back his arm.

Ethan Wright smiled at her reaction. "You're as squeamish as your mother. I wouldn't waste my time with you if you weren't useful. One more job and I'll take you home to Kansas. Won't you like that? I'm going to kill your mother and the old man and let you watch."

Clammy with fear, she froze in place.

He shoved by her and went to the desk. He pulled his billfold out and ruffled through the papers in the drawer, then jerked them out and dropped them on the flat surface. "Where is it?" He muttered and slid them one by one.

Laura watched him.

Ethan raised his head and narrowed his eyes at her. "It was there last night. Where is your box, Laura?" He marched over and grabbed her by the upper arms where the bruises wouldn't show. His fingers dug into her soft skin.

She cried out. "I…set it…down… at the market."

"Why?" His voice thundered in the small hotel room.

She stared at him. When she didn't answer, he shook her and threw her toward the bathroom.

She went in willingly and stood behind the door as he locked her in. *The bathrooms are all the same.* She sat on the edge of the bathtub as a lone tear trailed down her cheek. Maybe the lady would find the things inside and send help. She looked nice and smart. The reassuring weight of the flip phone tugged at her pocket. She'd slid it out of the puzzle box at the market when he wasn't looking. Now she waited.

~

Ethan Wright ambled toward the vendor next door to where the woodworker's booth was yesterday. His jaw clenched in anger as he realized it was empty. He checked his watch. *Maybe he was running late?*

"Good morning. Are you looking for Jake? He's not here today." A vendor nearby sidled next to him.

I can see that, you stupid cow. But he flipped on the charm for the middle-aged woman standing at his side. "I saw a little box on one of his tables that my wife would like."

Her smile faded and an uncertain look flashed in her eyes. "He's usually not here except for weekends. He's got a little shop in Indigo Alley across town."

"Indigo Alley, huh? I'll find it." He whirled and stalked off.

The woman took her phone out of her pocket and dialed. "Jake, it's Mona. There was a man at your booth. He's coming your way. He kind of gave me the creeps, if you know what I mean… Profits aren't everything….Just be careful, okay?" She hung up and watched the man stride toward the exit.

~

Jake pushed his cell phone off and thought about his sales from yesterday. All were to people he knew except the auburn-haired beauty and the little puzzle box that wasn't his. He went to the counter and pulled out his receipt box. He'd sold it for twenty-five measly bucks. He scribbled 'resort' on the bottom. She wouldn't be a return customer. With a shrug, he set the receipts back inside. Twenty-five bucks of pure profit wasn't bad anyway. Donning his denim apron, he walked back to varnishing the bureau he'd purchased last week. With gloves on, he set to work.

When the bell rang on the door, Jake set his brush aside and ambled to the front of the shop. A white man in his early forties with graying brown hair strode to the counter.

"Hello. Can I help you?"

"I'm looking for the little box that you sold yesterday from your booth."

Jake stiffened as he sensed the evil before him. The man's eyes lacked soul. No wonder Mona called. A tingle of fear inched down his spine. "Oh, was that yours? It was mixed with my stuff, so I thought my helper added it. I got twenty-five dollars for it. I'll pay you back." The cash box was in the bottom of the counter. He pulled off his gloves and knelt to unlock the lid. His fingers reached inside and took out a twenty and a five from the stack. He pushed the lid down and stood with the money in his palm.

The man pushed his hand away with his gloved one. "I don't want the money. I want the box. Who bought it?"

Jake's eyes leveled on the cold blue ones staring at him. His hand dropped to the shelf below to reach for the keys on his cell phone. He slid his fingers onto the smooth surface and pressed. The beep when he touched the first button echoed in the room.

"Don't be stupid." The man pulled out a shiny gun from his pocket and leaned forward to press it on Jake's forehead. "Who bought it?"

Jake's hands shook as he reached for the receipt box. The man grabbed the box out of his hand, stepped back, and pulled the trigger. Now he had the name of the purchaser.

Chapter Five

W e're headed to the beach," Katie announced as the four women finished breakfast. "Do you and Selena want to go? Amelia needs some sun. She's pretty pale. No, wait a minute, she spotted the lifeguard at the beach."

Amelia stuck her tongue out.

"Not I," said Selena. "I don't want to be a lobster for the wedding. Red hair and sun don't mix."

Haylie laughed. "Me neither. A nap is calling my name."

"Okay, party poopers. We'll meet you for a late lunch then."

Selena glanced at her watch when she and Haylie exited the elevator at their floor. Michael's scan should be done by now.

Haylie yawned. "I'm pooped."

"Are you feeling okay?"

"Yes. Just tired for some reason, and a nap would help. I guess I've been running too much."

Selena opened their door to find the room in shambles. With a gasp, she stopped in the doorway. "No, Haylie. Don't come in. We need security."

"Oh, man. What a mess. Is my dress okay? Can you see it?"

Selena nodded. "It's still hanging on the door and your shoes are on the floor."

"Thank goodness. I'll find the maid and report this."

She returned shortly with a man in a dark suit.

"Miss Simmons, I'm John Clark, the head of security." He reached out his hand and Selena shook it. "Mrs. Stevens told me you have a problem."

"Yes, sir. When we came back from breakfast a few minutes ago, I opened the door to find this mess. We had our valuables with us. Whoever did this wouldn't find too much except clothes and toiletries. Our plan was to be here until Sunday. We're here for a wedding on Saturday. Would it be too much trouble to get another room?"

"Not at all. If you ladies would go to the main reservations desk, I'll call down for you. We'll bring your things over after we conduct our investigation."

~

Michael stretched out his legs and opened his desktop as Dex sprawled in his spot in the sun. *Pops seems to like cheeseburgers and fries. I'll have to do that again.* He turned his link back onto the screen to check on Pops. He was still sound asleep in his chair, right where they'd left him. He clicked on his email to find Selena's report. He read the first part and then sat up straight.

Angel Townsend, 35, is what she says. Haylie knows her and the students love her—strict, but fair. She won a full-ride scholarship in D1 basketball at Notre Dame in college. Four-year player. Could have gone pro, but her dad diagnosed with early-onset Alzheimer's. Came home to take care of him. Her daughter, Laura, twelve-years-old, is also quite the athlete. Pops Townsend, seventy years of age, was a renowned basketball coach at one of the local high schools. Had lots of state championships. You know about the one in 1993☺. I couldn't find out

34

anything about the grandmother. She's been out of the picture for a long time.

Ethan Wright aka Murray, Salzburg, Morton is a different story. Killer-for-hire according to a couple of bureaus, even Scotland Yard. Suspect in numerous murders across the U.S. and across the pond. One profiler said he dresses according to the style of his victims. Another said he uses disguises. No confirmation of either. Last suspected of a trio of murders in the Northwest where he fit in with the logging crowd.

Shootings with the same signature—.44 with silencer from a left-handed shooter—in the last three months, businessmen or women working in either real estate or construction. String of four this time so far. Kellen Cooper (Oregon), James Roe (Colorado), Martha Reed (Tennessee), and Rolanda Wells (Georgia). Wells was killed last week. All were killed while at a convention. I'll attach police reports.

Wright's lawyer is missing and assumed dead. The judge who heard the case died three months ago from a sudden onset heart attack. I've asked my uncle to research the case on the legal end.

Just to keep you in the loop, Haylie and I are in a suite now. Someone broke into our other room. We'll tell Sam and Matt when they get here.

Let me know if you need anything else. I'll keep you posted on this end.

Selena

Michael saved the file and mused, "Why does he need the girl? Is he making her play some part in the killings? Or does he think she provides a screen when they travel? We need to find her quick before her usefulness ends."

He zoomed the screen on the camera feed to check on Pops before he called his former bureau chief. His stomach hurt to think that Pops had dementia or

Alzheimer's. It didn't look like dementia now. Pops, alert and smiling, was chatting on the phone.

Chapter Six

Selena turned the television down low and sat on the couch to work on the puzzle box. She rocked it back and forth in her palms and ran her fingers around the satin surface. She pushed with her pointer finger on each hand, rolled it over and stroked the bottom with her little fingers. The wood warmed in her hands as she worked with it. The two portions she'd slid out before popped away from the surface. Pushing from under those sections with her fingers, two more sections on the bottom brushed against the heels of her hands. She kneaded the inside of the box, and more sections moved. Turning the box over, she could hear something rattle inside it. She wasn't going to give up now. Chewing her bottom lip in concentration, she pushed with both thumbs and the top glided to the side. A drawer the width of a large index card two inches high slid out.

She set the box on the coffee table and grabbed tissues from the bathroom to guard the ends of her fingers. She unwrapped the first packet, a brass casing with Federal .400 circled on its end. *A spent bullet?* She set it in the middle of a tissue on the table.

Next was a tightly wrapped scroll of paper. She smoothed it, and names jumped out at her. It was a list.

A list of names that she'd found in her research, those names she'd just given Michael. Lines crossed out each one. There was an extra name on the bottom, but it was scribbled through and unreadable.

A murder list? The last item was a strip of paper tucked into the corner. She almost missed it. Written on one side was "785-220-2020," and on the other, "I love you, Mom. I'm sorry." *Laura Townsend's box.*

Her hands trembled as she dialed Sam's number first. It rang, then went directly to voice mail. She checked her watch and estimated the time. They should be just leaving on their connecting flight from Atlanta. Without leaving a message, she hung up.

Michael answered on the first ring. "Hi, Selena. Do you have more info for me?"

Selena explained about buying the puzzle box and her findings inside it. "I think Wright and Laura must be here. The resort has two large business conventions going on. Either fits the profile."

"Where are you?" He asked.

"We're in our suite, but we're supposed to go down for lunch in a little while."

"Stay there. I'm going to call my friend at the FBI to have him come pick up the box and the contents and get you some security. Your break-in yesterday may not have been random. Wright must know who you are. Whatever you do, don't leave the resort."

"Michael, we can't stay here. Kim's bachelorette party is tonight in a restaurant off the grounds."

"Listen to me, Selena. This guy won't hesitate to kill you for what he wants. Stay in the room until Bart gets there. I'll call you back when I reach him."

~

Sam and Matt settled into their seats on the plane. A heavy thunderstorm had them grounded for takeoff on the tarmac at Chicago's O'Hare.

"At least we're on the plane instead of stuck in the terminal," Sam sighed. "What's on the girls' agenda for tonight? Looks like we're going to be later than we planned."

Matt smiled. "Kim's bachelorette party is tonight. Haylie was grousing that it probably would consist of trying to keep the notorious Jocelyn out of precarious situations. Haylie said Selena had to use the contessa card at the dress shop earlier. She turned on the regal and convinced Jocelyn that another, more appropriate dress was classy. The one she picked out didn't cover everything. Even the shop owner was beside herself."

"That's my Selena."

"Got your ring?"

"Yep. In my pocket."

"Are you okay with the contessa thing and life as a count when you get married?"

Sam's eyes met Matt's. "All I know is we'll work it out. I love her and she loves me. It's part of her. She tries to keep Montaire separate."

"Attention, passengers. This is Captain Williams. We will be taking off as soon as we can. There is another storm behind this one. As soon as it passes, we will be on our way. Our estimated arrival time in Atlanta will be 7:17 p.m. Thank you for your patience. The flight attendants will be around with complimentary drinks."

~

Selena opened the door with the chain still attached.

"Miss Simmons, I'm Bart Dubois." The older man dressed in a dark suit flashed FBI credentials and appraised her with keen gray eyes. "Michael said you had some items for me."

Her hands shook as she pushed the door closed and pulled the chain to let him in. "Please come in and sit down."

Agent Dubois moved to the couch and sat near the

box on the coffee table. He slipped on gloves and glanced over the box and the items. "Michael forwarded the information you compiled on Murray, or Wright as you know him. We hadn't come up with the realtor/construction convention angle. That was helpful. Give me details on where you found the box."

Selena perched on the edge of the armchair opposite the couch. "Haylie and I went to the outdoor market. We were strolling through the woodworker's items and I spotted it. I've been working on it since then to open it. It's a puzzle box that opens when you touch it in the right sequence. I left it open for you. The items were there in the drawer.

"My fingerprints are on the outside, but I used a tissue when it opened. My fingerprints are on file in the government database as some of the research I do is classified."

He snapped his fingers and smiled. "Now I remember. Aegis Research Library. That's where I've seen you before. The last time we brought research in, the lady there told us she was a month behind and couldn't help us."

Selena's lips curled up at the edges. "I'm located at R & S Retrievals now."

"I've worked with Sam and Matt on cases before, and Michael was one of my agents. I'll take these items back to the lab. Michael said you're good at what you do." He rose, but hesitated at the door. "What's brought you to Florida?"

"A wedding. A friend's getting married at the resort on Saturday. The brides' party is tonight and we planned to go to town for that."

"Stay on the resort."

She nodded.

"Michael said he was concerned about your safety. A security detail will be in place for you shortly. Use common sense. Stay in your room as much as you can. Guard how you open your door."

"Haylie and I both appreciate that. Thank you."

"When do you plan to leave?"

"Sunday. Sam and Matt will be here later tonight."

"That takes away some security issues. We'll be in touch."

Chapter Seven

Michael knocked on the door at the Townsend house, and Pops waved him and Dex inside through the screen door. "What's up, Pops?"

"It's about time for Angel to come home from school. Laura told me she'd be here soon. Angel would rather I eat healthy all the time, but I sure liked my cheeseburger."

"That's good. I'll bring you another one soon."

The dog turned his head toward the garage at the sound of the chain on the opener rolling up.

Angel ambled inside. "Hi, Pops. How was your day?" She leaned down and gave him a peck on top of his head. She peered at Michael. "Is Donna here?"

"Not yet. You're early."

She turned back to her father. "Pops, did you like the casserole I fixed for lunch?"

"Didn't eat it so I don't know if I like it or not." He grinned. "I had a nice big cheeseburger with French fries and a vanilla milkshake. Boy, was it good."

"Where…?" Angel narrowed her eyes at Michael who shrugged.

"Not very healthy, but it sure tastes good every once in a while," Michael smiled.

"Thanks," she whispered.

"I've got some interesting footage to show you." When she sat beside him on the couch, he handed her his phone and clicked on the app.

Angel watched the video. "I'm sorry I didn't believe you, Michael. She hasn't been here all day."

"And I'm sorry I doubted you." He smiled. "We'll watch the rest later. I hear a car pulling up out front. What she did yesterday was come in, dump some of the casserole in the garbage disposal, and then come check on Pops."

Michael and Angel crept over to the doorway and watched as the blond woman shuffled inside, dropped her handbag on the counter, and headed directly to the refrigerator. She uncovered the casserole and sniffed, then pulled a tablespoon out of the drawer and dropped some of the casserole into the disposal. The spoon went into the casserole again, and she shoveled a portion into her mouth. After she took another bite, she slammed a cupboard door open, plucked something out of a plastic case and added it to the disposal, turned the water on, and flipped the switch.

"Pops' noon meds." Angel whispered.

Donna rinsed off the spoon, wiping it on her shirt, and put it in the drawer. She returned the casserole to the refrigerator and grabbed a can of soda. After glancing at Pops sitting in his chair, she plopped in one of the kitchen chairs.

Michael's eyes turned to Angel, her fists clenched at her side and her eyes blazed with anger. She took a calming breath and walked into the kitchen on shaky legs.

Donna climbed to her feet. "I'm sorry I didn't hear you come in, Angel. Pops had a pretty good day, though he slept quite a bit."

"Did he have a good lunch?" Angel bit the words off.

Michael followed her into the kitchen and noted Angel's eyes flash. *Uh-oh! She's going to deck her.*

Donna's eyes shifted from one to the other. "I guess he ate about what he normally does."

She wrapped her fingers around her purse strap tight enough to whiten her knuckles. "I need to get going as a friend has invited me out for supper. Can I have my check early? I know it's due next week but I have some bills that I'm a little behind on…"

"Why do you think you deserve your check early? And, why should you even expect a check for the services you render?" Angel's voice turned frosty. "I think not. How long have you left my father by himself?"

Michael stepped in. "Pops had a good lunch with me. He enjoyed it."

Angel's hands balled at her hips. "How long has it been since he had his meds at noon? You left him by himself."

Michael pointed at the camera in the kitchen.

Donna's face whitened.

"Don't come back. You're fired. What I suggest you do is find yourself a good lawyer. Maybe your friend who you're going out to supper with will loan you money for one, or the legal system can provide one. I really don't care. I'm pressing charges against you. If the woman at the agency is involved, she'd better get prepared too. Elder abuse is a serious crime, and believe me, I'm going to take it as far as I can. You don't do that to Pops, and you won't do it to anyone else. Get out."

The caretaker fled as fast as her flip-flops could carry her.

Michael sidled beside Angel. "Are you okay?"

Her green eyes flooded with tears. She shivered, and Michael moved closer.

He was lost at the sight of her tears. Wrapping his

long arms around her, he patted her back as she sobbed.

The flood finally subsided, and Angel backed away. "I'm so sorry. I didn't mean to do that. Everything with Laura and Pops has snowballed. I feel so helpless." She took a deep breath, then lifted her chin. "Have you found anything on Laura yet?"

"Laura called me today. She's coming home soon." Pops announced by the door.

"Pops, remember she's at camp right now..." Angel started.

A text popped up on Michael's phone from Dubois. "Bullet matches same caliber and striations of the shell that killed Rolanda Wells of Georgia. Confirmation of the other victims will happen soon. The phone number listed is of A. Townsend. Call is from a flip phone with the number 785-220-2020. Fingerprints on the items in the box were from one person unidentified. The shell casing had two fingerprints, one the same as on the box and the other was positively identified as Murray. Plane will pick you up at nine at KCI."

His eyes met Angel's. "Pops talked on the phone this afternoon. It was a little further on the tape." He clicked on the app and fast forwarded until that point. "The video didn't pick up the voice on the other end. Do you know this number 785-220-2020?"

"That's Laura's number." Her eyes rounded. "Have you found her? Is she alright?" She grasped Michael's arm.

"Selena bought a little box in the open-air market near where they are staying. It contained some items in it, including a note with your telephone number on it. Your ex-husband's fingerprints were found on it as well as an unknown juvenile's."

"Laura loves that puzzle box. Pops made it for her. She wouldn't leave it unless something happened to her..." Angel put her face in her hands. "Does that mean she's dead?"

"Laura said she was coming home soon," Pops repeated.

"Not at all. It just means that Laura and her dad may be in that area, and she's trying to get help. The box was on a table in the market. My old FBI boss wants me to go there as I know more about your ex than anyone else does. My plane leaves at nine from KCI. I've got to go home, grab my bag and drop Dex off with a friend."

Pops said, "Dex can stay here till you get back."

Angel nodded, "I'm on a week break until summer school starts, if they find funding. I'll be here with Pops." Her eyes locked on Michael's. "Please find my daughter."

Chapter Eight

"Darn it, Kim. I forgot to pick up my shoes at the bridal shop this morning," Amelia moaned. "What time is the photographer here to meet with you and Tommy? I know I promised I'd be there to help."

"She'll be here in about fifteen minutes." Kim glanced at her watch.

Kim, Kathy, the bridesmaids, and Selena had just finished lunch and were waiting for their receipts.

"We can pick them up," Haylie volunteered. "The guys won't be here for a while yet."

Selena bit her lip and didn't say anything. Her eyes went to the man sitting in a booth nearby. She'd picked him out when they entered the restaurant, and he followed them at a discreet distance. He looked tough and had scary eyes. Nobody would dare hurt them with him on security. Surely he could follow them when they made a quick trip down the road. She didn't want to scare Haylie, so she hadn't told her what Michael or Dubois said.

Amelia sighed. "You're lifesavers. I know this meeting will take longer than we planned, and the shop will be closed by then. Tomorrow we won't have time. Setup for the rehearsal supper and wedding will be an

47

all-day affair because the Masters boys will be no help."

*****

After the valet brought the red car to the portico and they slid inside, Haylie gazed over at Selena. "It was okay I offered us to get the shoes, wasn't it? You've been quiet since we left the suite. Are you okay?"

Selena peered around, checking for the man from the restaurant, but she didn't spot him. She glanced back to her friend. "I'm fine. I opened the little box."

"And…," Haylie urged.

"I found items that are related to the Townsend case inside, and they could be used to convict Wright. The girl and her father may be in the area and the box may be Laura's. Our break-in may be related. Michael didn't want us to leave the resort."

"Holy moly." Haylie chewed on her fingernail. "I threw us into it, didn't I? Should we just forget about it and have them couriered over?"

"Michael's former boss with the FBI came for the box when you were asleep, and he said they would provide security for us until the guys get here. I think I spotted one of them in the restaurant, and he's probably waiting in a car for us. No, let's get the shoes and then beat it back here."

Haylie pulled out of the lot and turned toward the shop. She weaved in and out of traffic, and a short time later, they parked in the little strip mall where Miss Jones waited.

"Thank you so much for stepping in yesterday," Miss Jones smiled at Selena. "Are you really a contessa?"

"I am. But, my friends call me Selena. I like that blue dress from yesterday. Do you have it in my size?"

Haylie's worried look faded into a grin.

"I think Sam might like it." Selena's eyes sparkled. "I could wear it to the wedding…Nah. That's not too regal to upset a bridesmaid."

The two friends spent a fun hour trying on clothes and visiting with Miss Jones, forgetting about Wright and their security.

"You are so ornery. I think you've been around Katie too long." Haylie clicked the door lock on the Lamborghini and slipped inside.

Selena leaned forward and pushed the lever to fold her seat down so she could lay her dress in the back seat. But, the back seat wasn't empty.

A man, the same man from the restaurant, and the same man she thought was on their security detail, leveled a shiny pistol at her.

"Get in and don't say a word," he growled.

Selena pushed the seat back upright.

"Start the car and drive west," the man hissed, "and don't turn around."

"Who are you," Selena asked, "and what do you want with us? This isn't our car; it's just a rental, so it won't bother us for you to have it. If you just let us go…" She folded the dress on her lap. Her hands slipped under the plastic covering her dress toward her pocket where she'd dropped her cellphone, then slowly pulled it toward her lap. *Sam and Matt should be here soon. If I can reach my phone, I can hit the tracker app Toby set us up with…* Her eyes met Haylie's scared ones.

"There's no need for you to know what I want. I'm not a car thief. Drive." He waved the end of the gun between them.

Haylie drew in a deep breath and put her hand on the gear shift. She glanced over her shoulder to check for oncoming traffic and eased out of the stall. Her hands clenched the wheel.

"Do what he says, Haylie." Selena whispered, "It'll be okay."

"Where's the box?" He growled.

"What box?" Selena pretended. *That's got to be Ethan Wright. Great. Murder magnet is active again. Sam always tells me I attract crazies.* She squirmed in her seat as her phone slipped on the plastic. She tried to grab it, but it slid between the seats. With a breath of frustration, she said, "Oh, that puzzle box. I couldn't get it open, so I left it on the table."

"It wasn't in your room."

"Our room was broken into," Haylie blurted. "The hotel moved us to another one. Someone must have taken it." She lifted her eyes and checked in the rearview mirror as she merged into traffic.

Selena caught the lift of Haylie's eyebrows. The police or their security detail must be behind them. She nodded.

The seat rustled behind them as the man shifted his weight.

Selena sucked in a quick breath as the muzzle of the gun was cold against her neck.

"Don't either of you get cute. If you get the cop's attention, you're the first one to die, red."

He chuckled. "Take the next exit, then turn right."

Darkness had fallen and the street lights were becoming farther and farther apart. The area where they were driving was rundown. Bars covered the windows of the businesses nearby.

Selena slid her left hand into the crevice, leaning toward Haylie. Her fingers brushed the edge of the phone, but they couldn't quite reach it. *Come on. Just a little more. Stretch, Selena!*

"Where are we going?" Haylie asked. "If we go too much farther, we'll probably need gas. I'm under a quarter of a tank."

The man yanked Selena's hair. "What are you doing, red? What do you have down there?" He pulled her head back by the hair and shoved her toward the glass. "Don't try that again."

"Mister, are there any gas stations near?" Haylie asked and winced as his fingers wrapped around her shoulder and squeezed as he leaned up to look at the gauge.

"We have enough to get by for a while. Turn left at the motel and drive around to the end and park."

Selena shivered as the car came to a stop in the back of a dilapidated motel. Rickety steps led to the second floor where the windows were blocked with plywood. *What now? There's some lights on in the office...*

"Get out, red, and put your hands on the top of the roof. Remember I have my gun aiming at your friend." The man wove his fingers into Haylie's long blond hair. "You, get out slowly."

She watched Haylie put one foot out as he pushed the seat down, bringing her head back as he crawled out of the back seat. He butted his door closed. "Okay, red. Move to room 35." He herded them across the broken sidewalk to the room a few doors down from the corner of the building.

"Open the door."

Selena looked around the dingy room, with Haylie and the man close at her heels. Loose sections of wallpaper drooped over the wainscoting on the walls as a musty odor seeped into her nose. Brown splotches from old leaks dotted the ceiling. With each step she took, dust motes from the threadbare carpeting wafted into the air.

One exit. Probably the only one. She slid to a stop in the middle of the room.

"Keep going to the bathroom." He waved the gun at them and stepped back. "Unlock the door."

With shaky fingers Selena slid the lock and grabbed the knob. *Why is this slide bolt here? And on the outside?* She swung the door open to find a young girl, elbows on knobby knees sitting on the edge of the bathtub, watching them with frightened eyes.

"Get in there. She's not smart enough to bite. I'll finish this when I get back." He smirked and locked them in. "I've got to see someone right now."

Selena listened at the door as Wright shoved the bolt closed. Her brows raised as water gurgled at the sink, and something skittered across the counter.

"He's taking off his makeup," the girl said softly, then her face crumbled. She glanced at Haylie and then dropped her gaze to the floor.

Chapter Nine

Selena mouthed, "Laura Townsend?"

Haylie nodded and sat on the edge of the bathtub by the girl. "Laura? Do you remember me?"

"Yes, Ma'am," The girl whispered. "You teach with my mom."

"That's right. I'm one of the kindergarten teachers. Are you alright, Laura?"

Laura nodded.

"Can you look at me? I want to see your eyes."

Laura raised her head, and shame colored her face. "It's all my fault," she whispered. "I shouldn't have left Pops' box for your friend to find. He'll kill you like he did the others."

"Not if we can help it," Selena said. "I'm Selena, and we're going to find a way out of here before your father comes back."

A spark of hope flickered in Laura's eyes. "I just want to go home to my mom and Pops. My dad locks me in when he... does his job, then he comes back, and we move on. But, this time he said it's his last job... He's taking me back home so I can watch him kill Mom and Pops." The spark sputtered and went out.

Selena smoothed the girl's hair with her palm, and

her eyes met Haylie's. "We won't let that happen. Let's figure out how to get out of here." She glanced around the narrow space, only wide enough to house the old rusty bathtub and toilet. "Did your dad attach a slide lock on the bathroom every place you went, Laura?"

"Yes, after the second city. He'd do that so he could leave me during the day. When we went to Denver, the door frame was broken, and I tried to escape the room so I could go home." She wiped the tears running down her cheek with her t-shirt. "That was when he told me he was going to kill Mom and Pops if I tried again. Before that, he told me we were on vacation and I believed him."

"I'm sorry this happened, Laura," Haylie pulled the girl into her arms.

"I caused it all. I thought Mom didn't want me to have a dad like the other kids. I wrote to him. That's why he knew where we were. Mom was scared of him. We moved a lot, changing our name, always on the run.

"Then, Pops got sick. He doesn't remember things. We moved back to his old house in the neighborhood where everybody knew her. She was Angel Townsend again and finished her school at night so she could teach. He hadn't looked for her... she fought hard to keep him away, but once he found us..."

"What happened?" Haylie asked.

The young girl stared at her hands. "I was stupid. I thought he loved me. He took Mom to court. The judge gave him visitation—first once a month, then every other weekend without hearing her side. Then, Dad took me and left. I didn't know he was a monster. He used me to meet certain people, but I think he killed them. At least he did the lady in Georgia. She was kind..." A torrent of tears fell then. All Selena and Haylie could do was watch them fall until her eyes drooped closed.

"She's asleep, Selena. I can't imagine the terror he's

put her through. We've got to get out of here. Hopefully, you have a plan," Haylie whispered.

"Not yet," she admitted. *Sam, I need you. It looks so hopeless. The only way out is locked.*

"I wonder if the monster even fed her?" Haylie worried. "Poor kid. She looks so thin. The last time I saw her she was shooting baskets with some of Angel's fourth graders. Surely her so-called father didn't…you know."

"No, I don't think he did anything besides keep her from her mom and use her to lure his victims in." Selena hoped she was right. "I don't know about you, but the edge of this bathtub has molded a right angle into my bottom side." She stood and looked around the room. "This door is the only way out. Too bad it opens into the bathroom. No window." *Wait a minute. There's something off with the door. The bottom peg has moved up, if I can pop it and the other two pegs out, maybe we have a chance.* She fell to her knees and lifted with her thumb and first finger. It slid a half an inch.

Haylie leaned over her shoulder. "Can I help?"

"I'm thinking if we can pry the pegs out, then when he unlocks the door it'll fall in. Then, maybe we can smack him with the curtain rod."

"I'll take the rod down, if you help me lay Laura down." Haylie grabbed a dry towel with one hand and balanced the girl upright with her other arm. "Maybe the bathtub?"

Selena nodded and shifted Laura's legs inside the tub. "I don't think her legs are long enough to reach the dripping faucet and rusty drain when we lean her against the back."

They eased her down and Haylie laid the towel under her head. Laura sighed in her sleep and curled against the towel.

"She's kind of warm, Selena. I wonder if she's

getting sick. We need to get her away from that monster."

Selena nodded, and both set to work.

"The boys are probably worried sick. I wish I'd have been able to grab my phone, but Wright wouldn't let me bring my purse." Haylie stepped up on the tub side to take the shower curtain down. "Too bad there's only one rod. We could hide behind the curtain and smack him from the side."

A grin flickered across Selena's face. *Or scare the dickens out of him when we popped out. Two angry women and a child...* "Our phones are both in the car. Maybe Toby can help Sam and Matt track him."

"When do you think Wright will be back?" Haylie's eyes met Selena's.

"I don't know, but hopefully Sam and Matt will find us first."

Haylie tucked the plastic curtain behind the toilet and tugged on the rod as Selena popped the peg out and set it on the sink. But try as hard as Selena could, the other pegs were rusted into the hinges and wouldn't pop up without tools. They sat on the floor and leaned against the side of the tub to wait.

Chapter Ten

S am glanced at his messages as soon as they landed in Orlando. Darkness had fallen. Selena's latest text was sent around two-thirty in the afternoon. "We just finished lunch with the rowdy bunch. Fried chicken salad this time. Sounds like tonight will be no-holds-barred. Kim is already worried about what Katie's promising. What I do know is plans are to start in the bar section on the resort around seven. Haylie and I have to go pick up some shoes at the dress shop before then. Love you. Can't wait to see you."

He texted back. "Just arrived in Orlando. Renting a vehicle and heading your way. I have something for you. I can't wait." He felt his inside pocket for the little box and took a deep breath as an odd sensation fluttered in his stomach.

~

The crowd at the reservation desk was lined up as Sam and Matt arrived at Palm Keys around eight. They dropped their luggage off with the concierge to hold until they could have the girls let them into the rooms. Then they moved to a sitting area where it was quiet enough to call.

Sam called Selena. The phone rang until it rolled over into the message system. He hung up and dialed again. This time he left a message. "We're here. Tell us where you're at." *Surely she would have texted, but there's nothing after the one from the afternoon. What if she can't answer for some reason?* He glared at his phone.

Matt's sober eyes met his.

"I can't reach Selena," Sam stated. "Does Haylie answer?"

"No. Her phone must be off. It just goes to voice mail," Matt admitted. "I'm starting to wonder. They were supposed to leave a message for us about where to meet them. That's not like Haylie at all. We're late, but they should be in the middle of the bachelorette party. I'm going to call Kim." He dialed a number and put it on speaker phone. Kim picked up right away, loud music playing in the background.

"Hey, Matt. Where have you kidnapped Haylie? She and Selena were picking up Amelia's shoes and were supposed to be here two hours ago… No, Katie. I'm not going to sing karaoke…You've got to be kidding. I've got to go, Matt." She giggled. "They're plotting against me."

Sam's eyes met Matt's worried ones. "What's going on? Where are they?" His cell phone rang. "Michael," he told Matt. "Hello, Michael. What's going on?"

"I've been trying to reach you. I'm in route to the resort, FBI transit. Selena bought a puzzle box when they were shopping yesterday. When she got it open, it contained some items that pertain to the Townsend kidnapping. Bart Dubois had them tested at the FBI lab there. The box definitely belongs to Laura Townsend. Fingerprints on a shell casing in it positively identify Ethan Murray, and the striations match victims murdered in the last month. There was also a list of those killed with the names crossed off with one more we can't read. I'm afraid Selena and Haylie may be in Murray's sights.

Someone trashed their room last night."

Sam sucked in a breath. "We're at the resort. Selena and Haylie aren't anywhere to be found. They didn't show up at the bachelorette party. Their phones are off. Call when you get here."

"That's not good. Dubois is in the loop. He's the one who wanted me down there, and he was supposed to provide security for them."

"Text me the contact information. We'll be in touch." Sam's eyes met Matt's. "The girls are in trouble. Michael is concerned that Ethan Murray's involved." He dialed Dubois as soon as Michael's text cleared.

The agent answered on the first ring. "Dubois."

Sam set his phone on speaker. "This is Sam Russell. Michael Rickard gave me your number. Matt and I worked with you on a case not so long ago."

"I remember. Russell, have you heard from Miss Simmons or Mrs. Stevens? They evidently lost the security man we had on them."

"No, we haven't heard from them. Their phones go directly to voice mail. My last text from Selena was sent around two-thirty."

"That's about the time our guys saw them driving away from the resort. Keep us posted if you hear anything from them."

Sam hung up.

Matt's hands clenched. "Between my wife and your girl, trouble has a way of finding them. What do we do from here?"

"Toby." Sam snapped his fingers. "Didn't Toby say his app could trace even with the phone off?"

"Yeah. He did."

Sam dialed.

"Hello, this is Toby. Leave me a message and I'll get back to you."

He waited for the tone. "Toby, it's Sam. Selena and

Haylie are missing. Can you use your app and trace them? I'm afraid they're in danger, again. Don't say anything to Will yet until we know what's going on." He hung up, and his phone rang a few seconds later.

"Sam, sorry I didn't pick up. Screening my calls. Hab a nasty code and fever. What's up?"

"Sorry you're sick, Toby. It's an emergency. Selena and Haylie may be tangled up with a killer-for-hire this time." Sam's voice dropped.

"I'll call you right back."

Matt paced. "Haylie hasn't been feeling well lately. Something's wrong. I finally convinced her to go to the doctor when she gets home…"

"They'll be all right. Between the two of them, they're pretty resourceful," Sam tried to convince himself, too. "Maybe we should track where they went. At least that will give us something to start on." He scrolled back over his texts. "They ate here at a restaurant that serves salads."

"O-Markins. Haylie mentioned it the first night. She was griping about guys trying to buy them drinks," Matt said.

"Selena didn't mention that," Sam grinned. "In Selena's last message, she said they had to pick up Amelia's shoes."

"If they had to leave the resort, they would have taken their rental." Matt stood still. "Haylie described it to me—a five-speed, cherry-red Lamborghini that handles like a dream and takes off on a dime with an awesome GPS. And knowing those two, it would be valet parked."

Sam nodded. "Maybe one of the valets knows if the car is still here. Let's head that way and find out."

The valet at the stand smiled when Sam asked about the girls and the car. "I worked two shifts today and I pulled it up for them. Nice ladies. They left around three, and I haven't seen them come back. I watched as they turned left out of the drive, headed toward town. Is something wrong?"

"Is it possible one of the other valets re-parked it for them?" Sam asked.

"No. It was me and Julio working today. Miss Selena talks to Julio about computers. He would have said something if he saw them."

Sam and Matt thanked him and moved toward the lot where their rental sedan was parked. "I guess it's safe to assume they aren't in the resort," Matt said. "Now I wonder if they

reached the dress shop. Haylie called it Jones' Formal Fashions, I think. It was near that outside market that's on the billboards. Maybe we can see if the shop's still open or they have a number to call on the door."

A short time later, they pulled up in front of the store and parked. An older woman was adjusting a veil on a young woman in a wedding dress as two other ladies watched.

"We may have lucked out," Sam said. "The light's still on and there's people there."

The two men strode to the door and found it locked. The older lady excused herself from the other women and walked to the door.

"Can I help you gentlemen?" She asked through the glass.

Sam held up a picture of Selena. "Have you seen this woman today?"

"Or this one?" Matt flipped his wallet open.

"That's Selena and Haylie. Why are you looking for them?" Curious, the woman narrowed her eyes. "Who are you? And why do you want to know?"

"Haylie's my wife," Matt said and flipped his wallet open again to show his PI's license. "We can't find them and hope you can help us."

"For goodness sake. They left here about four. I thought it was strange they turned left out of the lot. There's nothing out there except an old hotel or two and factories and shops. I got busy and didn't see the fancy red car return this way. I hope they're okay."

Chapter Twelve

There's too much ground here to cover." Matt drew a deep breath. They had pulled into an old hotel's parking lot. Few cars were parked around it, but a neon 'op n' flashed in the window of the office. "They could be anywhere."

Sam nodded. "Hopefully Toby will get back to us soon. If Murray has them, they're in big trouble."

Both men jumped when Sam's phone rang.

Sam held the phone out when he was greeted with a fit of coughing on the other end of the line. "Is that you, Toby?"

"Selena's phone is moving," Toby whispered. "On global mapping the car is moving up I-49."

Matt inserted, "It's going back the other way. Do you think the girls are in there?"

"I think we need to check it out." Sam cranked the wheel of the sedan, spinning sand under the tires and trailing it over the cracked pavement. "We're heading that way, Toby. Let us know when we're getting close. You sound terrible."

"Just like I feel…"

Sam drove a few streets, then merged onto the

freeway as Matt scouted around them.

"Selena rented a red Lamborghini, didn't she?" Matt asked. "There's one ahead in the passing lane."

Sam sped up enough so they could make out the lone figure in the car ahead, and then he dropped back to tail him at a distance. "One male passenger," he spoke tersely. "Do we have the right vehicle, Toby?"

"Yes."

A slow semi was ahead of them. Sam flipped his blinker on to pass, but couldn't when a gray van sped around them. He followed the van as soon as it passed, but the Lamborghini veered off.

"The car's heading toward a strip mall," Toby rasped.

"The dress shop's that way. Exit, Sam. That's probably where he's headed. Maybe the girls are in one of the vacant buildings there," Matt urged.

Sam parked in an empty stall at the back of the lot. "Looks like he changed vehicles or left. There's the car at the edge of the lot."

Matt nodded and reached up to the dome light and unscrewed the bulb, keeping the car dark when they opened the doors. He moved to the right toward the now-darkened dress shop, peering into each business for any light that wasn't on for security.

Sam trailed behind the cars toward the street. He paused in the shadows beside the broad trunk of a palm tree and listened, but the only sounds he heard was Matt's soft footsteps and the ocean breeze ruffling the fronds of the tree.

Matt turned toward the car and jogged to the driver's side door. He slipped his handkerchief from his pocket and pulled the handle. To his surprise the door opened. He hit the trunk button.

Sam ran to the passenger side, gun drawn, and peered into the small space as soon as he heard the responding click. "Empty trunk," he reported. He eased into the passenger seat and unfastened the clasp on the glove box, glancing in. "Just the rental agreement. The car's empty, Toby."

A hacking cough burst on the line, making Sam hold the phone out further to escape from the germs filtering through the air.

"Wait," Matt said. "Haylie's purse is on the floor under the driver's side." He opened the shiny shoulder bag with his fingers, shifting through the contents to pull out Haylie's billfold.

"There's one on the floor on this side too, probably Selena's," Sam's worried eyes met Matt's. "This proves they've been here, but, where are they?"

Toby whispered, "Sam, is there any phone chargers in the car? I can use the GPS system to track where the car's been. Plug your phone into the charging port. If the guy took them somewhere in this..."

"I've got mine in my pocket. Do your magic, Toby, and text us coordinates. Hopefully soon we'll let you rest. Maybe Michael can call in the troops to pick this car up."

"I'll call Michael. We'd better take the shoes and dress—probably for the wedding—with us." Matt threw the dress over his arm and slipped his fingers into the tie on the shoe's bag.

"It's downloaded on your phone, Sam."

"Thanks, Toby. Hopefully you can crash again."

A few minutes later, Sam tilted his head toward the edge of the parking lot where two patrol cars rolled in with lights flashing. "Here come the troops." He disconnected his phone, tucked the cord into his pocket, and pushed off the seat. A faint beep sounded under the seat. He reached his fingers in and yanked Selena's phone out.

As Matt reported to the officers, Sam's phone

pinged and then rang. He answered the call.

"Sam, it's Michael. There's a full alert at the resort, active shooter on the grounds."

"Is it Murray?" Sam tensed.

"They haven't got eyes on the perp yet. An off-duty officer was first on the scene and called it in. They're thinking robbery gone bad in the jewelry store by the canal. I don't think it's Murray. He's an assassin, not a thief. We're headed that way just in case. SWAT's been called in."

"Keep us in the loop. Toby's just texted us coordinates for the girls."

~

"I think I'm going to hogtie Selena, once we find them. I'm starting to believe she's a magnet for crazies." Sam gripped the wheel and zoomed around vehicles ahead of them.

Matt sighed. "And my wife aids and abets. Shouldn't kindergarten teachers be quiet role models for their students? But, no. She jumps in with both feet. Just as long as she's all right. Two hundred feet. Turn left."

Sam drove down a winding lane that led to a small filling station. "He must have needed gas. The gauge read under a quarter of a tank."

"Go to the right," Matt read.

"We're not too far from where we were earlier. Maybe we stopped too soon," Sam said.

"Turn left past the old motel."

Sam slowed to dodge clumps of weeds pushing through the cracks in the pavement and potholes. No cars lined the parking spots and no lights illuminated from the rooms on the back side of the hotel.

"Looks seedy. A perfect place to stow someone you don't want found."

"The dot shows the car stopped at the end room."

Sam pulled the sedan to the side of a dumpster and

parked. "Let's check it out." He drew his Ruger out of the side holster and slipped out from behind the wheel. Adrenalin spiked, and he slowed his breathing.

The door on the end room was ajar. Sam shoved the door open with his shoulder. The small space was empty except for two mattresses leaning against the wall.

The two tiptoed to the next door. This one was locked.

Matt leaned against the door. "I don't hear anything."

"No lights inside," Sam whispered as his partner pulled a pick out of his wallet and jiggled the door lock.

Matt's hand circled the knob and pushed the door open a crack. He pointed down with his first finger and crouched.

Sam nodded and whispered, "1-2-3."

They crept into the room.

Two full-size beds barely fit the narrow room. Numbers blinked on an old microwave. An older television filled the rickety desk. The air conditioner growled to life, and both men clenched their guns tighter. The only signs of occupancy were a man's suit swinging gently on the clothes rack, a dark suitcase across the luggage rack with items spilling onto the floor, and an unzipped purple duffle bag against the wall by the counter with its single sink.

Matt pointed to the closed door, to the little bathroom with a slide bolt fastening it on the outside.

Sam narrowed his eyes and stepped to the outer side. He took a deep breath and reached with his fingers to slide the lock. It opened with a snick of metal against metal. *Please God, let Selena and Haylie be in here and all right.* His palm slipped around the knob and twisted. He pushed the door open with the flat of his hand, and it thudded against the bathtub. All was still. The faded and cracked mirror reflected his outline as well as the shower curtain drawn across the tub. He took a cautious step inside the door and a slight rustle sent a shiver up his spine.

"Now!"

The curtain dropped, and Sam rolled on the floor with his gun aimed at the voice behind the curtain.

Selena stood above him, eyes blazing with fury, with a piece of the shower rod in her hand. Haylie backed her up with a metal pin from the door as a young girl cowered behind them.

"Haven't I told you that a shower rod is useless in a gun fight?" Sam whooshed out the breath he was holding. "They're here, Matt, armed and ready."

Chapter
Thirteen

Flow in the world did you find us?" Selena asked.

Sam rehung the shower curtain and locked the bathroom door behind him as Haylie helped Laura gather her things.

"Matt and I are that good." He glanced over at his partner and winked. "No, Toby locked on your phone in the snazzy red car, then he tracked the GPS here."

"We're ready," Haylie said, and they moved toward the door.

"Okay, ladies. We're going to take this slow and cautious. Wright may be waiting out there. Sam will take the lead, you follow, and I'll cover our tail," Matt said from his spot at the window.

Laura sobbed and sat heavily on the bed. "If I leave, he'll kill Mom and Pops."

Matt gently tipped her chin up. "I promise they will be safe. Trust us."

"If you stay, we'll have to stay, and I don't like the décor." Haylie said and took Laura's hand.

Selena wound her fingers through the duffle's straps, taking it from Laura. "It kind of smells in here too. I don't know about you, but I could use a cheeseburger about right now." A faint smile tracked across Laura's face.

Sam took one last look at Selena, then inched the door open and stepped out. Excruciating seconds passed as they waited.

Selena's eyes narrowed on the door knob as it turned. *Please God, let it be Sam.*

Sam stepped in and he leaned toward Selena and cupped her face in his hands. "Looks good. Car's clear. Let's go. Hug the wall. The car's on the other side."

~

Sam's phone rang when they were almost back to the resort. He glanced at the screen. Michael's name popped up. "Michael, we've got Selena, Haylie, and Laura Townsend. Wright locked them up in an old hotel. Everybody's okay."

"Wonderful. It's great to hear some good news for a chance. The shooter has been apprehended without incident. So, Murray's still in the wind. If only we could figure out the name that was scratched out on that list."

"Maybe Laura knows something. I'll ask and call you back." Sam shifted in the passenger seat. "Laura, you had things in the little box when Selena found it. The FBI has them. You were smart to hide them. That evidence will put your dad in prison probably for the rest of his life, and he'll never be able to hurt you, your mom, or your grandpa ever again."

She ducked her head into Haylie's shoulder.

"Do you know who he's stalking? If you know the name, we can protect them, just like we're protecting you till we get you home safe to your mom."

Haylie hugged Laura. "Honey, this will keep him from ever killing again."

Laura stiffened. "He's killed more than one?" Her voice rose.

"The FBI has traced him to at least four," Sam said

softly.

"He's a monster." She sniffed and wiped her tears on her sleeve. "He went to take a shower and I dug through his pockets. I only had a couple of seconds to get the paper out of his wallet. He looked at it a lot, so I knew it must be important. The names were crossed off with one line. I could read the name of the nice lady from Georgia, then the television had a news bulletin about her…"

"Rolanda Mills?" Sam asked.

She nodded and took a shaky breath. "He killed her. I knew I wasn't going to get away from him, but I had to do something. The bullet fell out of his pocket when I put his pants back on the suitcase, and it rolled under the dresser. The water stopped. I grabbed it even though there were spiderwebs. He was coming out of the bathroom… so I ran to the bed and hid the bullet under the pillow. I just made it under the covers. Later when he was asleep, I snuck them into my puzzle box."

"You think on it for a little while," Selena's eyes messaged Sam's warm brown ones. *That's all she can take right now, Sam.* "Matt, why don't you pull into that drive-in. I could use a hamburger and a soda. Maybe some food will help."

"Will I ever get my box back? Pops made it for me before he got sick."

Sam nodded at Selena. "I promise when we take you home, you'll have your box."

~

"I'm glad she ate a little," Haylie said as they drove down the street again. Laura was sound asleep with her head resting on Haylie's shoulder. "What's going to happen now?"

"Dubois will want to ask her some questions. It's clear she was forced into helping him. The girl will need some counseling to get over the trauma of being used to

71

kill people," Matt said.

"She'll get the help she needs," Selena murmured.

Sam nodded.

As they slowed to enter the resort, Laura woke up. "Rivers. I remember his name tag. The man was talking at the conference, and he stopped him in the hall so he could ask him a question even though we just got there. We waited for him. The man asked me if I liked sports like his son…"

"Very good, Laura," Sam said. "That will be helpful."

Matt dialed Michael and told him the news. He hung up and said, "Dubois will talk to Laura later in the room. They are searching the conferences right now for Rivers."

"I also need to get ready for the rehearsal supper. I don't want to spoil Kim's plans and make her worry."

"Let's grab our luggage and head to the rooms then," Sam suggested.

"Laura, Sam, and I will hang out and wait for Dubois," Selena said.

Chapter Fourteen

Wright glanced at his watch as he waited in the conference area. He needed to get his money and get out. The gray-haired porter visiting with a maid at the end of the hall may provide him opportunity. Rivers was lazy and his pattern was to return to his suite to retrieve his luggage after the session was over. The concierge would call the porter when Rivers was ready.

Wright waited until the maid moved away and then walked up to the porter. "Could you please help me? I seem to have locked my laptop in my room, and my wife has our only key."

"Yes, sir." The gray-haired man pulled his master pass card out and slipped it into the room's door, then stepped back as he opened it to a neatly arranged room, already prepared for the next guests. Suspicion clouded his eyes. "Are you sure this is your room, sir? It appears to have already been cleaned. Where would you have left the laptop?"

"Oh, yes. I'm sure. It's next to the bed." Wright pushed past him and walked around the corner toward the bathroom.

The man followed and the door swung closed behind him.

Wright waited for him by the bathroom door, slipping on his gloves, and wrapped his strong hands around the man's neck. He twisted until there was a slight pop and the man's body slipped down onto the carpet.

He pulled the porter's black vest off and dropped the body into the shower, drawing the curtain. Donning the vest in front of the mirror, he smoothed the gray wig. The porter's earpiece buzzed as he adjusted it deeper in his ear. He brushed a piece of lint off the vest and eased back into the hall. He was ready for the call.

Chapter Fifteen

W hat do you want for supper, Pops?" Angel asked as he ambled to his place at the kitchen table. "I suppose we could go get a hamburger and fries."

He grinned. "Maybe a cheeseburger this time."

"Michael spoiled you, didn't he? So much for us eating healthy tonight. We'll celebrate school being out for the summer."

Pops' eyes lit up. "Laura didn't call. Maybe she's on the way home."

Angel sighed. "I don't think her camp's quite over yet, Pops. I miss her too."

The telephone rang and she ran to answer. She didn't recognize the number on caller ID. "Hello."

"Angel, it's Matt Stevens. Laura is all right. We have her with us—Sam Russell, my partner, Selena Simmons, Haylie, and myself—We don't think he hurt her, but she's thin and scared. She'd like to talk to you."

Angel sank into the chair. "Oh, thank God."

"Mom?"

Angel grabbed the receiver with both hands. "Laura?"

"Can I come home? I said awful things to you…"

Tears streamed down Angel's face. "Where are you, honey? I'll come get you…just tell me where you are."

"I'm with Mrs. Stevens. They found me and took me away from the motel. I don't know where he is. He's a monster."

"Did he hurt you?" Angel's hands clenched into fists.

"No," the girl whispered. "He said he would kill you and Pops after this job is done. He's going to kill another man…"

Laura cried in the background, and it was all Angel could do not to break down herself.

Matt came back on the phone. "She'll be alright, Angel. We've got her under protection until your ex-husband is apprehended. It's close. The FBI is also providing security for you and Pops. They should be there anytime. Dex knows one of the detail, if you feel uncertain. They will show you their credentials when they come to the door."

~

Michael rubbed his eyes from the glare of the computer screen. The attendees' names on the spreadsheet morphed together. Laura told them the man's name was Rivers. He'd searched each of the three conventions, but no Rivers was to be found. *I've got to be missing something.* The room at the resort the FBI had borrowed was full of agents, and the hum of voices was loud, so he stepped out into the hall carrying the laptop. He sank to the floor after closing the door and pressed Selena's number.

"Selena, it's Michael."

"Did you find anything yet?"

"No. I'm coming up empty on the search. Each of the three conferences have over a hundred attendees, and I've tried everything. Now I'm down to variations of

Rivers. *Nada*. None of them fit."

The line was quiet. "You said attendees...Do you have the agendas? Could Rivers be a presenter?"

He drew his knees up and pulled the laptop in his lap. "Huh. I didn't think of that. No, on the list for Realty Force. There's a Candy Rivers listed on the program for Green Shores Ltd, but I'm assuming Candy would be female." He clicked on the third company. "Wait a minute. Jonathan Rivers is a presenter. He has to be the target. I remember him as a possible link to the Green Valley killings in Oregon... The bureau suspected him of being behind the killings, but couldn't find any proof. He had the most to gain. I've got to go. Thanks, Selena."

Michael ran back into the room and told Dubois what he'd found. Dubois sent details to the Green Shores conference rooms and the Construction Material Handling one. Soon the room cleared except for Michael and Dubois.

"Bart, Murray isn't going to go for the hit in a crowd. He's going to have everything planned so there won't be witnesses. My guess is he'll have Rivers isolated, maybe in or near his room. He's going to be disguised like a worker—a porter, a valet, or maintenance."

"Let's go. The presentations end at five. Rivers has a private plane, and he'll either leave straight away by car or head to his room. I'll cover the main exit."

Michael rode the elevator to the fifth floor. Rivers' room was in the block of rooms at the end of the hall. He checked exits first. *Murray will have his path planned for escape. With the elevator centered between two sections of rooms, I bet Murray will position himself closer to Rivers' room as late check-ins are arriving in the other section. Too many people. He'll use the stairs, not the elevator.*

"Rivers left the ballroom in the crowd. Unable to contain." A bass voice from one of the detail members spoke in his ear piece.

"Do you have eyes on him?" Dubois asked.

"Negative."

"Holmes here. Rivers is at the desk by the ballroom. Repeat. Rivers at desk."

"Make contact, Holmes."

"Negative. Crowd blocking my path. Rivers is moving toward the bank of elevators."

Dubois said, "Possibly coming your way, Michael."

"10-4, Bart."

"Reed and Jones, proceed to floor five east to back up Michael. Holmes, confirm Rivers' ride with the valet service. Stand by."

Michael stayed on the fringe of the new arrivals and scanned the area.

A gray-haired porter patted his pockets as he exited a guestroom by the stairs, speaking softly on a com. He strode out of the room, looking around him. He limped down the hall toward the elevators and the influx of guests.

A woman with multiple shopping bags waited impatiently as the porter approached. He picked up the suitcases, and she flounced toward Michael with her key card in hand, the scent of her perfume cloyingly sweet. The porter followed closely with his head down.

Michael caught a brief glimpse of the porter's face. A flesh-colored smudge marred the neck of his red vest. The gray hair was a wig, a good one. *A disguise or vanity?* Curious, he stepped closer. His eyes narrowed in on the back of the porter's head as he passed him. Dark hairs lined the back of the porter's neck. *He's not as old as he looks. Same height and build as Murray. Could it be him?*

The woman opened a door nearby.

The porter set the cases inside and turned to leave. He tucked her tip in his pocket and drawled, "Thank you, ma'am."

Michael stiffened. The last time he'd heard that voice was in a warehouse in Oregon...Murray's voice. He trailed the man's uneven gait with his eyes. *His wound from my gun must not have healed right.* Every part of his body ached to pull his gun out and keep pulling the trigger until the man lay at his feet, blood pooling out. But too many people were around to confront him now.

Murray limped back toward the crowd.

At least he hasn't recognized me yet. Michael moved to the other side of a cluster of guests, keeping Murray in sight. He whispered into his com, "Have eyes on him. Fifth floor east elevators. Dressed as a porter with gray hair and makeup. Too many civilians around to take him down."

"10-4."

"Rivers coming off elevator with another man. Murray glanced his way, then stayed busy with guests," Michael added. *Does Murray have an accomplice? Or is this part of his plan?*

As the crowd thinned, Michael squeezed into an alcove.

Murray pocketed the last of his tips and angled down the hall to the room Michael saw him come out of earlier. He pressed his fingers against his right ear before sliding the key card in the slot.

Ear bud? Was he awaiting directions? Or did he have a com on the FBI's signal? Michael shifted positions to stand behind a large potted plant where both doors were in his sight.

Rivers' door opened, and voices wafted down the hall. Rivers and his companion shook hands. The other man left the room and headed toward the elevator.

Rivers paused at the door, watching the man's back with a satisfied smile on his face. He pivoted and went back inside.

A tingle of adrenalin shot up Michael's spine. *Whatever was going to happen, Murray was not going to get away this time.*

Chapter
Sixteen

Murray's com buzzed, and a gravelly voice came on the line through the static, "Gino, Mr. Rivers is ready to have his luggage picked up in suite 525."

"Okay."

"What, no smart comment this time?" The voice chuckled.

"No." Murray stated, and he shifted his feet off the side of the bed. He checked his reflection in the bathroom mirror and leaned around the shower curtain to make sure Gino was still there. Then, he slowly opened the door and sauntered down the hall to Rivers' door. With a light knock, he called out, "Mr. Rivers, I'm here for your luggage."

Rivers opened the door and narrowed his eyes. "Wait, you're not Gino. What are you doing here, Murray?"

Murray pushed his way in and closed the door behind them.

Michael raced to the door to listen as Dubois came down the hall and nodded toward another one.

"Back door to the suite," Dubois whispered and slid

a key card in the slot by the door. As the two men slipped inside, the voices argued from the front of the suite. Dubois flipped his com to record.

"Where is the money you promised to have in my account, Rivers? I finished the hit in Georgia over a week ago."

"I've been busy with the conference and haven't had time."

Michael and Dubois inched toward the sitting room and the voices.

"I want it now. I don't like how you do things. I don't meet face-to-face with clients, but you insisted." Murray's words were clipped. "I don't leave witnesses."

"I paid you well. You have nothing to complain about. You already killed three people because the sheik's sons ordered them." Rivers said. "What's one more? She was a big thorn in my side. I was tired of her demands. I'll pay you, I said. Put that gun away, you fool."

Michael held up one finger, two, and three. Then the two burst into the sitting room. "FBI. Raise your hands!"

Rivers reached for his pocket and fired at Murray. Murray swung his gun toward the others and pulled the trigger, aiming center mass at Dubois.

"Gun!" Michael shouted and shoved Dubois to the side.

Murray squeezed off another shot and ran for the door.

"He's mine," Michael shouted and took off after him as other agents burst in.

The hallway was empty.

Michael swung his Glock from side to side and inched forward. A trail of blood drops dotted the carpet, leading him by closed doors. Step by step he moved on. The whisper of a breath behind him froze him in place. He turned his head slightly to see Dubois. He whooshed out a quiet breath and pointed down at the spots.

Dubois nodded.

The spreading red path led to the room where Murray had come out of minutes before.

Michael gestured low and wrapped his fingers around the knob. The lock held.

Dubois slid the card inside, making the light flash green.

"FBI!" They shouted and burst inside.

Murray was face down near the bed with his gun on the floor inches away from his outstretched hand. Blood pooled around him.

Michael kicked the gun away and flipped Murray on his back.

His eyes stared back. It was over.

Chapter
Seventeen

How does pizza and a movie sound, Laura? We can have a quiet evening just us three," Selena suggested. "Mr. and Mrs. Stevens will be back in a little while. They had to go to the rehearsal supper. You remember she told you she's the matron of honor at the wedding?"

Laura stared at her and nodded.

"Sam and I are pretty good company." *She's so scared. Hopefully for her sake this will be over soon.* "Sam likes cheeseburger pizza with lots of cheese. Is that okay for you with some soda?" Selena called room service, and forty minutes later, they sat on the sofa in front of the big screen television, scrolling through a movie list.

A knock came at the door, and Sam stood and felt for his gun at his side. "Michael. Agent Dubois. Come in. We're almost ready for one of the girls' chick flicks."

Laura glanced up, her eyes huge as she watched them enter. "Are you going to arrest me?" She whispered. "You're in Pops' book. He talks about you and said you are a cop now."

Michael knelt at her side. "I'm Michael. I work with

Sam and Matt now. I wanted to tell you that it's all over. Your dad won't ever hurt you again. A bad man shot and killed him. And no, you aren't going to jail."

"He's dead? Did he kill anybody else like he killed the lady in Georgia?" She bit her bottom lip as tears glistened in her eyes.

Dubois approached. "I'm Agent Dubois with the FBI. Michael's right. Your dad didn't kill anybody else. The evidence in your box would have put him in prison for a long time. You were a brave girl to leave that for Selena to find. Is it all right if I ask you a few questions?"

She nodded, and Selena took her hand.

"Can you tell me where else you've gone since you've been with your dad?"

"He—he told me we were on vacation, and we were going places he always wanted to see. We drove to Oregon first. He said, 'We're tracing where the pioneers went.' It was fun until I started thinking about my mom and Pops. I missed them so much. I told him I wanted to go home."

Tears rolled down her cheeks.

Selena squeezed her own eyes to keep from crying along.

"Then, he didn't try to be nice to me. He drove to the edge of the road in Colorado…and he laughed at me when I was afraid. It was so far to the bottom of the cliff. He laughed at me when I asked him to stop. He locked me in the bathroom in Tennessee when I wasn't with him. If I didn't do things when he said to do them, he'd hurt me. He'd grab my arm and pinch hard until I cried. I didn't care about that but he said he was going to kill Mom and Pops and make me watch."

Laura leaned against Selena's shoulder and sobbed.

Anger flashed in Michael's eyes. He took a deep breath and gently shifted a finger under Laura's chin to make her look at him. "It's over. He can't ever hurt you or them. Agent Dubois said I could take you home. Would you go with me? We can even ride on an FBI plane."

She raised her head. "Really? I can go home?"

"Whenever you're ready." He smiled.

Chapter Eighteen

L aura's home safe," Sam announced the next morning. "Michael said there were lots of tears, but happy ones. The bureau is going to provide a good counselor for her. As soon as this wedding is over, we can return to safety." His lips curved up in a smile for Selena.

"Well, we'd better hustle. Pictures start at eleven," Haylie said.

"You guys don't have to show up until it's time for the wedding," Selena suggested.

Matt laughed. "Do you think we'd let you girls out of our sight since you're trouble magnets?"

Haylie opened the door and a small paper carton with a lid fell inside. "It must be a wedding present that someone sent to the wrong place." She knelt to pick it up.

Matt grabbed her hand. "No, it's addressed to the Contessa Selena Carmichael-Simmons." His eyes met Sam's as they stood in the doorway.

"We'd better give Dubois a call. This is too much of a coincidence."

"Wait, the only people who know I'm here are the

members of the council." Selena mused. "Maybe Will Cardwell sent me something?"

Selena dialed Will, and he answered on the first ring. "Hi, Will. How are things in Montaire?" She nodded. "Great. By any chance did you or the council send me something here in Florida? What? Let me put you on speaker. Sam, Matt, and Haylie are here."

"No I didn't. I'm sorry to spoil your holiday," he said. Selena rolled her eyes. *Like it hasn't been eventful so far?* "Reynold Base is missing. We're starting to think foul play. Your package may be part of that."

"We're taking it inside, Will," Sam lifted the package with his fingertips and carried it to the coffee table.

"Be careful, mate."

"You girls, stay back."

Matt turned on his phone light and scanned the surface. "I'm not seeing any wires."

"I'm lifting the lid, Will." Sam pulled up an edge of the lid with his ink pen and flipped it on the floor. "There's a wooden box inside. I'm taking it out of the package."

The rectangular wooden box was a little larger than Laura's with sides of one piece of dark stained wood mitered together at the corners. The top was hinged and fastened at the front by a latch with a crest on the front.

Matt took a photo and emailed it to Will.

"Sam, I'm going to open the box," Selena insisted and pushed her way in. "It's addressed to me." *No, my love, you're not going to get blown up opening my box.*

She grabbed tissues, slid her fingers under the latch, and closed her eyes, waiting for the explosion. When nothing happened she opened them, squeezed the edges of the paper at the bottom between two fingers and set it on the coffee table. Cut out letters spelled out, 'Reynold Base will be dead unless 50,000 dollars is left under

Chatnam Pier by the Contessa at ten tonight. X on box. No cops.'

"It's a ransom note, Will," Sam said grimly. "Fifty thousand delivered by Selena by ten tonight."

Will let out a deep breath. "The Base family crest is on the box. What do you want to do, Selena? Do we pay the ransom?"

"Can we get that much together, Will?" Selena bit her bottom lip.

"Maybe."

Sam spoke up, "We've just worked with the FBI on a case. We can probably enlist their help rounding it up."

"The note says, 'No cops.' The FBI are cops," Selena said. "Why don't you see what funds you can raise, Will. The rest can be paper. My question is why Base? We need to research why he was picked. He has no ties to the international industries and is on the council because of family name only."

"Very well, Selena. I'll set this in motion and put Toby on the research."

"Sam and I can do the research on Base here as we have a few hours. You may need Toby for something else. The wedding begins at three."

"I'll keep in touch," Will said and punched off.

"I've got to go for wedding pictures." Haylie checked the clock on the wall. "Late. I can't hold them up."

"Go," Selena said. "There's nothing you can do right now."

Haylie slipped out the door and Matt followed.

Sam reached for the room phone. "I'll check with the porter service to see if one of them delivered the box." He dialed and hung up shortly after. "Negative. Someone else brought the box." He dialed Dubois and explained the new situation.

Dubois was on the fifth floor with the forensics

team, gathering evidence, so he was in the suite in minutes. "Our security cameras show a teenager at the door two hours ago. They're looking for him now. My guess is someone passed it to him for a quick buck."

As the men talked arrangements Selena ran to her bedroom for the laptop and set to work on the counter. She input some data and glanced at Sam. "Is the box merely a coincidence? Or are Angel, Laura, and Pops in danger?"

"Maybe we shouldn't take the chance." Sam's eyes met hers. "I'll call Michael and have him take them to the cabin."

She nodded and went back to work.

Ninety minutes later Sam rested a hand on Selena's shoulder. Dubois was gone. "The sandwiches I've ordered from room service are here. Let's swing to the couch and eat. We've got to go downstairs for the wedding. Find anything yet?"

Selena circled her head to get the kinks out, stretched, and smoothed her palm on the top of Sam's hand. "Lots of firewalls, but I finally broken through. Now, it's just a matter of time."

"You know I'm not going to let you deliver that money, don't you?" He murmured and put his arm around her.

She smiled. "We'll work it out. Base's life depends on it." Her laptop chimed.

"Wow," she said. "Base's financials are heavy in the red. I'll generate a report and forward it to Toby to delve deeper."

"I'll let Will know. The wedding starts in a few minutes." Sam grabbed her hand.

Chapter Nineteen

The ushers were seating the last guests when Selena and Sam arrived at the venue. White wooden chairs faced a curlicue-trimmed gazebo dressed with white roses, overlooking the ocean. Gentle waves soothed against the shore. A soft breeze ruffled Selena's hair and played with the hem of her new blue dress as they found the seats saved for them near the front. Selena took a deep breath and made herself focus on the wedding.

Sam took Selena's hand in his and smiled. "Pretty day for a wedding. Let's enjoy it."

She nodded as Matt sat down beside her.

The music began and the bridesmaids, escorted by the groomsmen, walked down the aisle.

Jocelyn swayed, dragging a red-faced Robert Masters, and peered into the crowd. For eligible men, no doubt.

Matt snorted and whispered to Selena, "He's a nice guy, ready to dump the prima donna on her head."

Selena wrinkled her nose. Steve Masters had eyes only for Katie Perkins it seemed, whom they followed. Her face glowed with his attention.

Hal Prine, the only non-brother of the groomsmen, and Amelia were smiling ear-to-ear.

Selena watched Matt turn and beam at Haylie as she walked by with Andy Masters. Her escort winked at her when she turned for her spot up front, and she punched his shoulder.

The music changed and Tommy Masters appeared at the front, waiting for his bride. Selena studied his face as Kim made her way toward him. Tears glistened in his eyes as he took her hand. *Will Sam think I'm the most beautiful woman in the world too when he's waiting for me?*

~

The wedding was over way too soon. As the crowd moved inside for the dinner, Sam shared the information Selena had found with Matt. The three of them found their place cards near the head table where the wedding party sat.

"Base is in deep trouble if he's involved in gambling. Some of the heavy hitters wouldn't hesitate to use any means to get their money." Matt said.

"The box is what has me puzzled," Selena met their eyes. "It's old and looks like it should be in a museum. Would someone take the trouble to steal the box before they kidnap Base?"

Sam asked. "Or do you think he's involved? What do you know about him?"

"I've gotten to know the council members pretty well. Base seems more interested in the most money for the coffers of the treasury than what's best for Montaire. He's the one who came up to us when the coronation ceremony was over and grumbled how much money was spent, even though most of the traditions had to be met, and I lowered the council's budget substantially. I hate to admit it, but he could easily be in on it."

Sam nodded. "He's the short man with the narrow

mustache?"

Selena smiled. "Yes. He would have access to a box with his family's crest, and his travel records show him visiting the United States frequently, supposedly on business. He would know I'm here and take advantage of that fact."

"What's our plan?" Matt asked.

~

Selena pressed the metal case against her chest and tucked the chiffon drape matching her dress around her shoulders. The quarter moon cast little light on the pier. Her sandals tapped on the wooden planks as she stepped around the trash on the pier. She hesitated about halfway to the end and wrapped her fingers around the rail. The twinkling lights around the gazebo and the reception area were fireflies in the dark. The shadows of the revelers glided on the dance floor. *Let's get this done so we can return to the fun.*

Step by step she drew closer to the wooden box marked with a black X painted on the side. Her heart pounded. Sam was in the water below the pier. If things went wrong, she was to dive into the crashing surf below. Matt lay on the roof of the closest lifeguard station with a high-powered rifle and night scope. Dubois was a com call away at the hotel on the helicopter pad.

Her fingers shook as she lifted the lid and slipped the case inside. The lid thudded against its base as it slipped from her hand. She spun around and headed back to the beach and the reception. Now, it was Toby's turn to track the case.

~

Sam dropped into the chair next to Selena, where she sat near the dance floor, and wrapped his arms around her. "You okay?"

She pulled his face close, kissed him, and took a

deep breath. "I was worried about you. The waves crashed hard against the pier, and all I could imagine was you getting hurled against the beams."

"No one has been near the box, according to Toby or Dubois."

Selena shifted to face him. "Does that mean they knew the case held only paper?"

Sam shrugged. "We'll let it play out. There's nothing we can do now besides wait." He pulled her to her feet. "The music's good. Let's have some fun while we do."

~

The weight of the little box in his pocket reminded Sam of what he planned to do. When the live band took a break, Sam took Selena's hand and led her away from the crowd toward the beach.

The waves whooshed against the sand and rolled back out, and the balmy breeze tossed its fingers in her hair. She leaned down and slipped her shoes off as they walked in the cool sand. The gazebo was in front of them and Sam pulled her up the steps with both hands. He cupped her face in his hands and leaned down for a kiss. "I wanted to ask you something while we were here. Would—"

A ping of wood snapped above them. Fear replaced romance, and Sam pushed her down to the deck. White rose petals rained around them as the rail on the ocean side splintered.

"Sam, what's happening?" Selena struggled to sit, but he held her down.

"Stay down, Selena." He pulled out his phone. "Dubois, Selena and I are in the gazebo. Somebody is shooting at us. Send help."

Chapter Twenty

S am, please sit. You're driving me crazy." Selena seized his arm to make him stop pacing in the sitting room of the suite. "If they'd wanted to hurt us, they could have, but they didn't. Neither of the shots were close to us."

He turned and looked at her, lines forming on his forehead. "I could have gotten us killed. I was too busy thinking about the night and you." *The ring feels like it weighs a ton in my pocket. Is the time ever going to be right to give it to her?*

"That's not so bad, is it?" She punched him. "You can't say we've had a boring week or I'm boring." She reached for the room phone. "I'm going to order pizza. I bet you twenty bucks that Haylie will be hungry too when they get back."

The door clicked from a card, and Matt and Haylie rushed in.

Haylie rolled her eyes at Selena. "Are you having excitement without me? Matt filled me in, and I'm glad I was a matron of honor at the time. Kim was in such a haze she didn't notice that Matt and you guys were missing. I'm just glad you and Sam weren't hurt." She walked to the mini-refrigerator and opened it. "Do we have any snacks left over from last night?"

Matt eyes met Sam's and dropped to Selena's hand.

Sam shook his head.

Matt pulled his tie off and plopped on the couch. "I'm going to have to put a room service order in or Haylie won't wind down. The wedding dinner looked pretty good when it was being served. Of course that's when we left. Do you guys want anything?"

"We're ahead of you," Selena smiled.

~

Dubois arrived at the same time as the pizza. Once they sat around the coffee table, he pulled a slice out of the box. "The shots were a diversion. The techs made a preliminary scan. The shooter wasn't planning to hurt you or Selena. They found a rubber bullet lodged in the latticework of a trellis. If the shots had hit you, they would've stung, but not killed you."

"Does that mean the case is gone?" Sam asked.

"Yes."

"Then, they know it was filled with paper," Selena said. "Have we killed Base?" Tears glistened in her eyes.

Sam took her hand. "Remember what Will told you. The council made the decision not to pay the ransom. It's not on you."

She nodded

~

Early the next morning, Selena entered more data in her laptop as the others slept. *Somehow Base and Ethan Wright must connect. Laura Townsend's father has one more killing before they return to Kansas. What if it isn't Jonathan Rivers that's crossed off the list? Maybe Rivers is only part of it and he isn't supposed to be the last victim.* She took another sip of coffee and leaned back in the chair.

Toby said Base is deeply in debt last night. Selena

downloaded the spreadsheet and highlighted the unusual items—over and above taxes, bills, and everyday expenses. She clicked on a government-travel listing to see if and when he'd been to the United States. The highlighted items matched the flags on his visa. Numerous business trips mostly to Las Vegas, and the expenditures for those days had higher amounts—ten thousand, twenty-five thousand, five thousand, twenty thousand. *Las Vegas. That's interesting. Is he in debt to someone there?*

She knew Base well enough to know she didn't like him. The council meetings were busy, and their topics were Montaire-related. Base was a member because of tradition. He didn't own or run any of the international companies or local business for that matter. She pulled up her dossier file on the council members to find out what he did.

Reynold Base, son of Edmund and Margaretta (Base) Helmund, born January 2, 1975, was named to the Council of Montaire on March 2, 1990, upon the death of his grandfather, Telmar Base. He is given an allotment of funds monthly from the Base foundation trust. No other source of income.

Selena tapped Will's number on her cell. "Will, it's Selena... No, we haven't heard any more this morning. No contact from the kidnapper as of yet. I've got some questions about Reynold Base. Do you know if he's a gambler? ...Not that you've heard of? Okay. How about any interests in real estate or construction?"

Sam ran his fingers down her cheek. He mouthed, "About ready for breakfast?"

She nodded, and a gleam of satisfaction crossed her face. "Bingo. Have Toby look into any rumors of who the competitor is. I'll get back to you in a while." She hung up and her eyes met Sam's. "I know the connection. Wright's next-and-last victim was to be either Base or a competitor for construction of a new resort in Las Vegas, and the fifty-thousand-dollar ransom was to pay for the hit. The resort once constructed will be worth 102 million dollars. All we have to do is wait for the next ransom contact."

Sam's eyes deepened to almost black. "I don't think we'll get another ransom demand. Our best possibility would be to go to Las Vegas and look into things on that end."

Chapter
Twenty-One

A ngel shot the basketball at the net at the other end of the concrete slab. Pops watched from a lawn chair in the shade with Dex at his feet. Laura, with her legs curled up under her, watched listless. Pops laughed as the ball pinged off the rim, and Michael's hands retrieved it before it could roll on the grass. "That's E, Michael. I thought I'd be more competition. Laura, why don't you beat him in H-O-R-S-E instead of me? That way I can bring lunch out to the table."

"No thanks," the girl whispered.

Angel glanced at Michael before she looked at Laura. "Why, honey? You're so good at it."

"Not anymore. I'm not good at anything."

Dex growled.

"What's wrong?" Angel asked.

"We need to go in the house," Michael said. "Hurry. Something's not right. The house is more secure."

"Laura, help me with Pops," Angel ordered as she clasped one of Pops' arms.

Laura helped as Dex's ruff stood at the back of his neck with his eyes staring toward the drive.

"Are we still going to play basketball?" Pops asked. "I like to watch. Michael was schooling Angel. His jump shot is an arrow, but he wouldn't have beat you, Laura."

"I'll trounce him later, Pops."

Michael locked the door behind them as Dex trotted to the front of the great room, ears on alert. The perimeter alarm lit up on the security panel. "Everybody, move to the storage room in the back. Hurry." He drew out his gun from his shoulder harness and signaled the dog to stand by the door.

Two men dressed in jeans exited a blue pickup with fishing poles in the back. Both men were bulky in build and hard-looking. The older man had pockmarked skin and whispered to the other. Michael picked him out as the one in charge. *New jeans on both. Coincidence? Not hardly.* He peered over his shoulder to make sure the door to the back was closed.

The doorbell pealed.

Michael headed to the door to give security stationed in the woods time enough to approach the house. He opened the door, but left the chain attached. "Hello. Can I help you?"

The older one spoke, "Sorry to bother you, but we're looking for some friends of ours. We were supposed to meet them to do some fishing on Milford Lake."

"You're a long way from Milford. It's about forty miles east of here."

"Could we please use your phone? Hank doesn't have one and mine is dead."

Michael nodded, reached up in a ruse to unlock the chain, then pointed his gun at the older man. "Now," he shouted.

Four security men ran out of the woods, guns drawn.

The older man put his hands up, but the other pulled his gun out.

"I wouldn't do that if I were you," Michael said.

"Drop it or your boss is toast."

The man narrowed his eyes, measuring the pluck of the man with the gun. He dropped his pistol in the dirt and raised his hands.

The two men were secured, and minutes later, county police and highway patrol pulled into the driveway with sirens screaming.

Michael knocked on the safe room door. "You can come out now. Laura, do you recognize either one of the men?"

Laura's eyes flashed as she approached the door and peered out. "No." She squared her shoulders. "No, I've never seen either of them before. Were they after my mom and Pops? Nobody is going to ever try to hurt them again. Even if I have to shoot them myself." Her words trailed off at the end.

"Between you and me, kid, we're not going to let that happen," Michael promised.

~

Sam found the message from Michael when they landed in Denver. He played it back on speaker phone.

"This is Michael. Security was breeched at the cabin, but we're all okay. Two men are in custody, and cops say they're local muscle. One of them spilled they were just looking for Selena. A short man with a European accent gave them five hundred apiece to snatch her."

Selena said, "Looks like that clenches Base's involvement. He's five-feet-four inches tall and has a heavy accent. Las Vegas should give us answers."

Chapter Twenty-Two

The Cessna touched down at McCarren International Airport around dusk, and Reynold Base hurried through the gate into the concourse. He couldn't waste any time. The two men he'd hired at the cabin had failed him and were in police custody. He should have known the Contessa was not there.

He squinted in the bright lights as he hailed a taxi outside the terminal. Time was running out before the Contessa and the men she worked with found him. With deep regret, his plan to fake his kidnapping for Murray's fee backfired in his face. Instead Murray got himself killed over the woman in Georgia, Rivers' addition to the list. At least the idiot didn't know about the resort plans to squeal to the cops. His mouth twisted into a grimace. Rivers' time was numbered in custody. An expatriate from Montaire gladly accepted the drugs he'd promised.

His silent partners expected him to finish the transaction on the resort. He would have to get rid of the competition himself with Murray's backup gun. He almost relished the thought as Ralph Jackson negotiated as dirty as he did and met him with other ruthless demands.

The deal was to be closed this morning. If he didn't finish it as expected, he became disposable. He'd made mistakes, mistakes that could get him killed, but maybe the sheik would trade them for the Contessa. With her long auburn hair and smooth white skin and title, she would bring a good price. At the least she'd be a convincing bargaining chip for his freedom.

~

Base slipped on his leather gloves before he broke the gun down on the dingy hotel bedspread and oiled the pieces, wiping the excess on a threadbare towel from the bathroom. He buffed it with the soft cloth he'd found in the metal suitcase and carefully refit the pieces. After adding the clip, Base replaced the gun in its foam holder inside the case, and snapped it shut. Easing his arms inside his European suit coat over his silk shirt, he picked up the case. He was ready, and the building was a short walk around the block.

His Italian loafers carried him down the well-worn carpet toward Jackson's office. The beat-up, three-legged table, covered with a silk flower arrangement, stood guard on the quiet hall. Few people worked in the building and any witnesses would be away at lunch. He shoved the flowers back with the case and flipped the catch open to pull out the gun. His hands shook as he aimed it at Jackson's door, then let himself in.

Jackson sat behind his desk. A self-satisfied smile lit his face. "I've been expecting you. You're too late. The land was sold an hour ago to a local investor."

"No!" Base roared in anger and fired. The bullet struck the wall behind Jackson.

Jackson returned fire with the pistol he held beneath his desk.

Base twitched, expecting a move by Jackson, but lost his balance and landed on one knee, taking him out of the line of fire and saving his life. He snapped off another shot, and this time Jackson slumped in his chair.

The smell of cordite coated the top of his mouth as Base ran from the room, plucked the case from the table, and shoved the stair door open with his shoulder. He took two steps at a time until he reached the third-floor landing where he peeked out in the hall, stopping only to see if there were any witnesses, then exited toward the elevators. His heart raced as he replaced the gun in its case as the elevator descended to the lobby. He forced himself to a normal gait toward the building's doors— the image of a businessman leaving from a meeting. When the hot air struck his face, he pulled in a deep breath. Now all he could do was run. He failed.

A dark limousine rolled up to the curb. The back door opened, and a deep voice said, "Get in."

Chapter
Twenty-Three

The Boeing 747 queued up to land at Las Vegas. Soon Sam, Selena, Matt, and Haylie walked through the concourse toward the luggage area.

"All the hype about landing at night to see the lights is true," Selena said. "It's brighter than noon. I think our first plan should be to check into a suite to establish our base of operations, then get some rest until daylight. Will should be arriving in a few hours."

Sam agreed.

"We could all do with some food and a shower, too. Especially in that order," Haylie quipped.

Matt grinned and pulled his wife toward him. "Don't tell me you're hungry again."

Selena pulled out her phone to check their reservations. "The Regency Palms has a shuttle service and an all-night buffet, so we should be set."

~

Selena's cell phone buzzed when she came out of the bathroom, towel wrapped around her damp auburn hair.

Toby's name popped up on the screen. "We're at the airport, Selena. Will thought you might need some extra help and brought me along. It wasn't a hard sell; I don't like Base anyway."

She laughed. "You sound better today. How'd you get rid of your crud?"

"I finally gave up and drank some of my newest stout. It must have killed the germs, or they're anesthetized.

"On another note, I found out about the ransom box. Base 'borrowed' it from an antique shop in Montaire. It's over a hundred years old and needs to be in a museum. It's not the first time he's taken things and favored someone with them as gifts. The crest is a new addition. He must have been watching you when you bought the puzzle box and thought he could get your attention with it. My guess is he stole it for another reason and then wanted the money for himself.

"I've also tracked him back to a consortium in Abu Dhabi. They are heavy into construction of million-dollar resorts, with the reputation of making their competition disappear. They also like to take American women home with them, if you know what I mean. Homeland Security has at least two people from Abu Dhabi coming to Las Vegas on business in the past week."

Selena shivered. "That means we need to find him before they do. I've arranged lodging for you, Will, and the others here at the Regency Palms. We'll see you soon." She disconnected.

Haylie came out of her room and headed toward the refrigerator. "Is there any ginger ale or pop in here?"

"Why? Are you feeling sick? You look pale," Selena said.

Haylie admitted, "I'm a little queasy. Is anyone else feeling bad? Could it be something I ate?" She grasped the back of a chair and held on.

Selena pushed her into the chair. "I'm not sure if it's

the food. We ate about the same thing on the buffet. Maybe we need to get you checked out," she said. "When we did wedding things this week, you tired out fast, which isn't like you at all."

~

A dazed Matt sauntered into the ER's waiting room a short time later. "It's nothing serious," he said, "but she wants to see you two."

"Are you okay, Haylie?" Selena asked as they entered the partitioned room.

Haylie grinned as Matt took her hand. "We wanted to tell you together. It seems like there is a little Stevens on the way. The doctor's tests confirmed it."

"What? Congratulations!" Sam clapped Matt on the shoulder as Selena hugged Haylie. "That's awesome."

"When we get home and you get rested up, we'll have to have a baby shower to end all baby showers," Selena said. "And, you and Matt are going home as soon as the doctor says you can. Las Vegas isn't safe right now."

"But, Selena, you and Sam might need us…"

"No buts. You need time to adjust to your news. You can't help any more on this case except to brainstorm, in case we've missed something. Will and Toby will provide any extra bodies we need."

Chapter
Twenty-Four

*N*o! No! He can't stay in there. Let him out! He'll
*die in the heat. Please, I'll do anything, anything
you say. It's me you want."*

*Selena's body was coated with perspiration and her
hair straggled around her face.*

The man laughed with his back to her.

*The sun beat down. Down on the sedan's trunk. Sam
was locked in there.*

*The man wanted her to beg, but he had to turn
around so he could see her beg.*

*She ran to him on wobbly legs, but they were caught
around her. She kicked, but the cocoon wouldn't let her
free. She rolled over, but the silken threads pulled
tighter. Her arms were bound under her, and she opened
her eyes to see...Reynold Base.*

*Base spun around with a red stain coloring his shirt.
Black holes gleamed from his eyes on his white face and
words spewed out of his mouth. "You didn't pay, so
Russell will have to." He set fire to the trunk.*

"No!" she screamed. "Sam!"

"Selena, honey, wake up. You're having a
nightmare." Sam pulled her into his arms.

She forced her eyes open and searched his face. "I thought I'd lost you." She pulled him close with shaky arms.

"It must have been a doozy. I could hear you thrashing around from the sitting room."

"I'm okay," she sat up. "This needs to be over soon."

Sam's eyes met hers. "It will be. Dubois has permission from the doctor to interview Rivers. Maybe he'll know something to help us."

Rivers did. He'd overheard an argument Base had on his cell phone. Jackson was a real estate agent in downtown Las Vegas.

~

"I have the address. Jackson's office is in the Tucker Building. I'll email you the coordinates to your cells," Toby said.

"What do you want us to do while we wait for you and Will?" Selena asked.

"Look into Jackson, his business associates, financials, and any connection to Base," Sam said.

"Please be careful," Selena kissed Sam goodbye and smiled at Will.

"I'll take the financials and associates if you look into the connection with Base." Toby propped his feet on the coffee table and pulled his laptop on his lap.

~

The Tucker Building sat silent in the Nevada heat. Sandy grit piled into the corners of the entryway and trash littered the cracked-and-pitted stone flooring. Sam and Will spotted the building directory, or what was left of it, by the elevators, and plastic push-in bulletin board letters listed the remaining tenants.

"This must be it," Sam said. "Jackson Realty, floor five."

"I wouldn't think they'd have too many clients the

way this property looks."

Will nodded. "Not too many occupants either."

The floor shook as the elevator rose to five.

Jackson Realty was the only occupied office on the fifth floor. Tepid air greeted the two men as they strode down the narrow hall. The office door was open and they walked in. The stained drapes rustled from the forced air of a revolving fan. A tall, dead plant sat forlornly in front of the windows. Dust coated the top of an old reception desk skirted by three office chairs.

Sam drew his Ruger out of the holster and Will followed suit, sweeping the outer office quickly as there wasn't much to see. As Will circled the desk, a hum came from behind a closed door. "Here," he whispered.

Sam took high and Will burst in low. An old computer rumbled on the desk in front of them. An older man with a brown comb-over lay behind the desk on the floor, blood spreading from the hole in his chest.

Sam snapped a picture and texted it to Toby for identification. Almost immediately his phone pinged. "It's Jackson."

Will pulled the desk drawers open with gloved fingers. A paper lay face down in the middle drawer. He grasped it by the corners and laid it on the desk top. "A signed deed for this area of buildings dated today, and it looks like Jackson signed it over to Commodity Ltd.," he said.

Sam moved closer to see, and a sticky note caught on his shoe. "What's this?"

Will leaned over and plucked it off. "It has Reynold Base's name on it as a representative of Bahrein Manufacturing with an amount. Wait, the amounts are different."

"I've got a bad feeling about this. Base is too close of a tie to Selena."

The two men took the stairs and called the murder

into the Las Vegas police after they left the building.

Chapter
Twenty-Five

Do you want something to eat or drink, Toby? I'm going to take a break and grab me a soda, so I'll get you one," Selena said.

"I'm good. I'm finding some deep stuff here. Base has been associated with this consortium for some time. I knew he was a weasel, but not to this extent." Toby's eyes glittered with the hunt, oblivious to the room around him.

Selena took her soda with her into the bedroom. Her phone beeped on the charger, and she glanced at caller ID to see Haylie's name pop up.

"We're home."

Selena keyed a response as she snuggled against the headboard, "Are you feeling better?"

"Yes, I'm fine. Matt will drive me crazy before this is over. He wouldn't let me do anything when we got home. It took him three trips to bring everything in. Of course, we stopped at the gift shop at the airport on the way to the truck. We now have a pink bear and a blue bear, just in case. I think I'll milk it while it lasts."

Selena laughed. "Of course, you will. All we've found out is that Base is involved with bad people from

Abu Dhabi. Toby's in his element."

"I'd better let you go. Matt's bringing me something to drink."

As Selena disconnected a heavy thud shook the floor. She tensed. The suite was too quiet. She slipped her shoes on, dropped her phone back on the charger, and called, "Toby? Did you hear that noise?"

Boy, he's really engrossed. Is that the way I get when I'm in search mode?

She picked up her empty can and headed for the sitting room.

Toby sprawled on the floor by the table with blood running from his hair to his face.

"Toby!" Selena screamed and ran to him.

"Hello, Contessa." Base.

She ignored her fear and knelt by Toby to feel for a pulse. *Thank God, there's one.* "If you'd have killed him, Base, you wouldn't have any place to hide." She straightened Toby's arm that was bent under him at a strange angle. "What do you want? Your money? Sorry, but the principality of Montaire has never paid traitors and will never do so."

She turned to stare at Base and noticed a heavy-set man she didn't recognize standing behind him.

"No, Contessa. I don't want the money. It was only to pay for Murray's responsibility for Jackson's other client. You see, you are going to make payment for me to the sheik. He doesn't forgive mistakes. My freedom in exchange for you."

"Never," Selena hissed.

The man's eyes glittered. "The sheik likes women with fire. This one won't easily be broken. It's too bad I can't sample before him, but he would know."

A dart of fear flashed between her shoulder blades.

Base tugged her roughly to her feet.

She yanked her arm back. "Toby needs medical

help. Let me call someone to help him."

The other man closed in, and Selena was sandwiched between the two men. He pulled her left hand up and caressed it before moving it over to his jacket, pressing her knuckles against the gun in its holster. "If you say anything to anyone as we walk out of here, I will pull this gun and shoot anyone in sight. Do you understand?"

All Selena could do was nod.

The three of them moved out the door of the suite and down the hall. One of the maids stood a few doors down and glanced up ready to talk to Selena.

Don't say anything, Maria. Just tell Sam I was acting strange and who I was with. Please, please, go to the suite next. Call help for Toby. Selena hoped Maria read her body language. She stared toward the elevators as her feet dragged on the carpet with the man close to her side.

The elevator doors opened, and Base pushed the button.

The lobby was full. Business people milled around outside the ballroom near the lobby, waiting for the doors of their meeting to open. Tourists prepared for their day at the casinos and other attractions. Guests lined up to register or check out.

Selena's heart pounded as she searched for someone to help. She willed Sam and Will to walk through the automatic doors.

The man pressed her against his side, and the leather holster and hard gun bruised her ribs.

She didn't need the reminder. *Please God, let nothing happen here.*

Slowly, they wound through the crowd. Step by painful step, Selena was forced closer to the outside and to the dark limousine parked at the curb.

The fear in her eyes must have given her away. The

concierge stepped up and asked, "Good morning, Ma'am. Do you need a taxi?"

"No."

The man squeezed his fingers around her upper arm until she winced.

"No, we don't need a ride. My husband has one prepared for us. Thank you anyway." Selena forced her lips into a smile. *Don't try anything. He'll kill you and others. Just tell Sam.*

They walked across the sidewalk toward a dark limo. Selena could feel the concierge's eyes staring at them as Base pushed past the valet, yanked the back door open and disappeared inside. The other man's large hand pushed Selena into the back seat beside a third man, then jogged to the front seat.

~

The valet stood on the sidewalk and watched as the car rolled away. He muttered the tag number under his breath.

"Did you get it?" His boss asked.

"Yes."

Chapter
Twenty-Six

When Sam and Will arrived back at the hotel a short time later, police cars with mars lights flashing lined the street, and an ambulance idled at the edge of the portico awning. As they walked into the hotel, the concierge and a man in a suit jacket broke away from a small group of police and strode toward them.

"Mr. Russell, I'm glad you're back. This is Detective Jonas of the Las Vegas Police Department. Someone has taken Miss Selena," the concierge burst out. "Two men marched her through the lobby."

"When?" Sam asked.

"About twenty minutes ago."

"Your friend said they broke into your suite and knocked him unconscious. He said she wouldn't have gone unless they'd forced her to." Jonas reported. "We are looking into the incident."

"Is Toby hurt?" Will asked.

"He has a cut on his head, but has refused to go to the hospital. Who are you, sir?"

"I'm Will Cardwell, one of the members of the Montaire Council. Were you aware that Selena is the

116

Contessa Selena Carmichael-Simmons of Montaire and this is an international incident?" Will squared his shoulders and stared at the detective.

Sam narrowed his eyes to measure his own opinion of the detective. Will's impression of people was usually right, and his body language said he didn't think much of Jonas.

"The Las Vegas police are quite capable of handling this situation, and we would like to ask you to step down right now," Jonas said. "We are well aware of your agency, Mr. Russell. Please let the professionals handle this."

Sam forced back his temper, nodded, and turned toward the elevator. "Very well. We can be found in our suite."

Will glowered at the detective and followed.

One of the valets sidled next to them as they waited for the elevator. "My boss said to give you this." He slipped Sam a scrap of paper with a license plate written on it. "It was a black limo. Maria, one of the maids from your floor, will meet you there. She saw them leave and knew something was wrong. Sorry about the clandestine stuff, but we've dealt with Jonas before. Let any of the floor staff know if you have questions. We all hope Miss Selena's all right."

An EMT was wrapping gauze around Toby's head when they entered the suite as her partner waited.

"You okay, Toby?" Sam asked.

"Yeah, I'm okay. I've had harder boinks on the head, but they bleed like stink," he growled. "No, I don't want to go have tests at the hospital."

The EMT smiled and packed up her gear. "Let us know if you change your mind."

"I won't."

As soon as the EMTs left, Toby turned, his eyes darting from Sam to Will. "I'm so mad at myself. The men just waltzed in and took her. I'm pretty certain Base was one of them. He smacked the back of my head with the vase on the floor. In the glimpse I had of the other guy, I'd never seen him before."

"It's not your fault," Sam said. "We've got a copy of the deed and names to research if you're up to it."

"It'll take me a few minutes to power up Selena's computer and get through her firewalls, but I can access my DropSite in Montaire. The creeps smashed my laptop. Hopefully they missed hers." He gazed forlornly at the debris on the floor.

Sam answered the knock on the door.

One of the maids stood nervously outside. "Are you Mr. Sam?"

Sam held the door open. "Yes, I'm Sam. Please come in."

"I'm Maria. I was cleaning at the end of the floor when two men took Miss Selena down the hall. I knew something was wrong as she and I have talked about things since she's been here."

"You're friends," Sam said.

"Yes. They held her tight between them. One was big. She didn't talk to me, just stared straight ahead. Her eyes looked scared."

"You said the one man was big. What did the other look like?"

"He was short like me but with slick hair. His suit was different."

Will held out his phone. "Is this one of the men?"

She nodded.

"Base," he confirmed.

"I have pictures here from the company you gave me, Sam." Toby spoke up from the counter. "Should she look at these too?"

The Bahrein Manufacturing main page was on Selena's screen with a group picture of employees in front of a tan sign, reading Bahrain Manufacturing. Palm trees stood as sentinels on the sides of the rectangular building as acres of sand spread as the backdrop.

"Can you enlarge the people, Toby?" Sam leaned closer.

Maria squinted as the images grew larger. "There," she said and pointed her finger at a man standing in the second row. "That's the big man."

Sam smiled at Maria. "You've helped more than you know. We have somewhere to look now. Thank you for your help." He walked her to the door and closed it behind her.

Will took a deep breath.

"We're in trouble here," Sam's eyes burned as he headed to the counter. "We need some help and not the detective downstairs. Do you think Dubois has a good contact here? We've got to stop them from leaving with Selena. If they get her out of the States, we may not get her back."

Chapter
Twenty-Seven

Selena scooted as far against the door as she could the second they drove away from the hotel. Her shoulder pressed against the door frame. *Where's the stupid handle?*

"I told you your father would like her for his harem, didn't I, Fatim?" Base asked from the seat facing them, his hands woven together so hard his fingers were white against his suit.

"She is quite beautiful," the man beside Selena answered and reached out a finger to stroke her face.

Selena stiffened. "You touch me again and I'll scratch your eyes out." She forced back the nausea ready to spew out of her mouth. *Harem? Am I to be some sheik's plaything? Sam, I need you. Where are you?*

The man laughed. "Father will enjoy her spirit, also."

Her hands fisted in her lap.

Fatim's eyes hardened as he glanced at Base. "You remember what he said about failure during the last meeting in Abu Dhabi?"

"I tried, Fatim. You know I did," Base whined. "I even killed Jackson. The hitman didn't finish his job, so

I had to… Cooper, Roe, and Reed, the competitors are all dead."

"You allowed Murray to add another to the list. Rivers' girlfriend, who was being too possessive, had nothing to do with the Las Vegas property," Fatim hissed. "That made our offer too late. You failed. You'll pay like Rivers did."

Selena watched as all the color faded from Base's face. *This is all related. Murray was Laura's father. How in the world could it happen?*

"Rivers is dead?" Base whispered. "But he's in jail in Florida…"

Fatim shrugged. He pushed a button on the console of his door, and the glass between the front seat and the back slid down. "Drive to the place we found last night."

"No!" Base shouted and leaned forward toward Fatim.

But the big man in the passenger seat swiveled around and slid his arm around Base's neck, forcing him against the seat.

Selena leaned forward and stared into Base's face. "I want to know why. You had a lucrative income from the Base trust, and you joined forces with evil. You betrayed your country and its traditions. Why?"

Bases' eyes turned icy and his nose flared. "I was never good enough. My grandfather controlled me from the time I was a child. How would you like to be fifty-three years old and paid a monthly stipend? My wife divorced me because I was cheap. And, you, Contessa, are illegitimate, not a true heir."

"Greed drove him to gamble in our casino," Fatim smirked. "We own him, so that's why he became our agent."

~

Selena watched out the window as the pavement and the city lights faded in the distance. The big car shuddered on the sandy road until it began to climb low sandstone ridges. When the climb was too steep, the driver stopped, raised the glass between the front and the back, and shut off the engine, leaving the headlights aiming at a rocky formation.

The driver opened Fatim's door, and he got out, pulling Selena with him.

Base cowered in the corner.

A shiver of fear flashed down Selena's spine. She glanced back at the seat to see the

big man slip out of the front seat, open the back door to yank Base up, and shove him out.

Base fell to his knees on the hard sand. He cried out, peering at Selena. "Help me, Contessa. Do something."

Sadly, there's nothing I can do. She lowered her eyes.

The big man and the driver dragged Base up the rise by his arms, scuffing his expensive Italian shoes on the sand and leaving two trails in his wake. He kicked and screamed.

Selena knotted her fists to keep from covering her ears. *Oh, God. Oh, God. They're going to kill him.* She took a step forward.

Fatim grabbed her arm.

When she shook it off, he pulled a small pistol from his pocket and leveled it at her. "Did you think I was helpless? Do not interfere. This is his fate he bought for himself."

Selena clamped her lips closed and stood on shaky knees, watching until the men were out of sight over the hill.

Seconds passed, and then a thud echoed across the dark.

She took a deep breath and squeezed her eyes shut. *I'm next. I love you, Sam. Don't mourn for me too long. Just. Be. Happy.*

Fatim poked her in the ribs with the barrel of the gun. "Get in. Now."

Chapter Twenty-Eight

S am's phone rang.

"It's Dubois. I'm sorry to tell you that Rivers is dead. Someone killed him in the holding cell. He was in solitary."

"We've got more to worry about here. Someone snatched Selena from the suite. One of the maids identified Base and a man who works for Sheik Abu Bahrein," Sam said.

"That's interesting. Murray would've run in Bahrein's circles. The sheik would have been able to pay for his services. He also uses a front man bound to him to make his real estate deals. Base would fit the bill. Homeland Security is very interested in Bahrein. His son, Fatim, is his eyes, and he travels with his friend, Amed Gehar, and another man. The sheik never leaves his compound. Hitmen like Murray kill off the likely competition beforehand. But, if the competition wins the deal, then Fatim and his two men kill the front man right away. If the deal happens, the front man is rewarded for a few days, then disappears."

"And what about—"

"If they have Selena, then Fatim will bring her to his

father as a prize. She is safe until that happens."

"And after."

A pause. "Women whom Fatim has delivered are never seen again."

Sam looked grimly at Will.

"Tell me what you need on my end," Dubois said.

"I got it," Toby announced from his spot on the sofa. "I've got the limo on the GPS monitor. There are four heat signatures in the vehicle—two in the front and two in the back—headed southeast toward town. I'll email the coordinates to your phones." He rubbed his head. "Get going. Find her."

As they raced to the door, the detective from downstairs had his hand up to knock on the door. "I need to talk to you," he blurted out as they shoved past him.

Will poked the elevator with his pinky. "Did you hear anything, Sam?"

"Nope."

~

Jonas followed the two men to the elevator, but the two steps behind made the difference as the door swept closed in front of him. He paced by the doors and jabbed the buttons several times. A man pushing his wife in her wheelchair waited for the elevator in front of them to open. The elevator door swished open and as the man pivoted to pull her in Jonas pushed in front of them, jabbing the Ground button. "This is closed for official business. Take the next elevator."

"My, what a rude man. Do you think we need to say anything to the hotel?"

Jonas grimaced, overhearing the lady's comment, as the door swished closed. He clicked on his phone, but the reception was spotty. He came out into the lobby with a red face, phone in one hand and notebook in the other. "Detective Jonas, badge 128. Put out an APB on a Sam Russell and Will Cardwell. Both white, approximately thirty years of age. Cardwell is a native from Montaire in Europe. Russell, U.S. citizen from Kansas. They are suspects in a kidnapping."

The voice broke in on the other end.

"They have what?" Jonas asked and fumed. Special clearance from the FBI outranked him. "I want the APB on them. Now. I want to know where they go." He jammed his thumb down to end the call.

~

"Sam, it's Toby. I think I know a possible destination. There's a small airport in the hills beyond McCarren. They would have come private. Homeland Security only has two arrivals this week from Abu Dhabi and they are a husband and wife. Dubois said the son travels with two men. I'll plot you a course. Put me on speaker."

"I owe you, Toby."

"I just pray we're not too late to stop them before they get off the ground with Selena aboard," Sam whispered and tromped on the gas.

Will's eyes flashed. "We will, mate."

"Turn right on Seventh. There's a traffic jam on the interstate."

Sam slid around the corner and punched the accelerator. The truck bounced on the rough street. Will balanced one hand on the ceiling to stay in place.

"Two miles, turn on Johnson."

"We're running out of road, Toby. There's a blockade at the end of the street before we can get to Johnson."

Will stared ahead. "There's a cart track to the right. Aim for that. But, you'd better slow a little for the bump."

The truck bounced into the air and landed on its tires. Sam slid around the curve and climbed up the bank on the other side.

"Where did you learn to drive, mate?" Will asked.

"That's what Selena always says," Sam grinned.

"You're good, Sam. This street angles off to the airport road. It might be a little rough as it's not well traveled." Toby said.

"Great," Will whooshed.

Sam slowed the truck as they entered the airport property and turned off the lights. He parked the truck behind an old hangar at the end of the lot.

The two men eased out of the truck and stalked forward. An older Cessna sat on blocks inside the old hangar. Sam's heart dropped. Did they come to the wrong place? That plane wasn't going anywhere.

They skirted around a small block building with 'Office' written on the side. Sam glanced through the plate glass window. Moonlight streamed in through the hole in the roof.

Will pointed at a newer hangar to the right. Fluorescent tubes illuminated a man's shadow moving back and forth in the light.

They hunkered down in the shadows as the hangar doors screeched open. The man in a uniform moved the block under the front wheel of a shiny Lear jet and pushed it out into the night.

"We beat them here," Will whispered.

The pilot moved around the plane and did preflight checks. When he finished outside, he dropped the steps. The cabin lights blinked on.

"Should we neutralize him first?" Sam asked.

"It's too late. They're here," Will said as a limo sped down the road toward the plane.

Chapter
Twenty-Nine

Selena leaned back against the leather seat, watching the stars. Heart heavy, she focused on the beauty of the night. The stars were so close in the desert. *Sam is probably searching for me. Oh, how I disliked him when they first met. Cocky, impetuous, a terrible driver, but fiercely protective of those he loves. He never got the chance to ask me to marry him, at least I hoped he would have. He tells me he loves me often enough.* Tears moistened her eyes, but she wouldn't let them fall. These men would not see her cry.

She bounced on the leather seat as the limo wheels navigated the rough pavement to a small airport in the desert. The first hangar was rusty, and its wall was buckled on one end. It was small enough that the bumper of a pickup parked on its side protruded a little in the dark. In the newer hangar, the lights were on and a flag hung limply on its roof. *The pickup probably belongs to someone in the larger hangar and, if they are here, they work for Fatim. Looks like I'm my only hope to get out of this mess.*

The limo curved around the building, and a shiny Lear jet awaited them with lights and engines on.

Her pulse raced as the driver turned off the motor and climbed out of the front seat. He opened Fatim's door and proceeded to the trunk. The thunk and rustle told her he was pulling the suitcases from the back. She cast a sideways glance in his direction. He lumbered to the plane with his hands full and climbed the steps of the plane.

Fatim slid out, headed to the back of the car, and retrieved a silver case from the back. He shut the lid and glanced up as the big man approached him. "Amed, we didn't end up with the property that we wanted, but this trip wasn't wasted. The pilot is prompt as usual."

"Your father will be pleased. May our friendship always last as well," the big man said.

Now's my chance. Go, Selena! With the dark tint of the windows, they couldn't see. She scrambled over the back-facing seat and dove over the front seat to a door that would open. The men were still at the back as their voices echoed in the night.

The pilot switched on the jet engines and they screamed to a deafening life.

She lifted the handle and swung a foot out onto the tarmac. A heady rush of hope swept over her when she crept outside. *This might work.* She turned to run to the shadows when Fatim seized her arm.

"What good is a prize if it can't be given?" He laughed. "Look, Amed. I have an escapee."

Selena struggled, but he was too strong.

Fatim pulled her toward the jet.

She kicked and scratched, anything to keep off that plane.

The big man stood at the steps with his hands on his hips, laughing. "What's the matter, Fatim? Can't you handle a wildcat?"

Fatim jerked her toward the plane.

She dropped her head and bit him as hard as she

could. The coppery smell of blood filled her nose. Fatim shoved her toward Amed. "You take her. She bit me."

Amed picked her up and flung her over his shoulder. "Go. I've got her." Fatim pushed around him, rubbing his arm, and climbed the stairs. Amed balanced her against his neck and took the first step.

A shot rang out.

Fire seared Amed's leg, and it buckled. He lost his balance and fell backward. Selena dropped to the ground and rolled to the side.

Another shot rang out and pinged against the fuselage of the jet. Fuel poured down the side of the plane.

"Amed, grab the woman and let's go," Fatim screamed from the door.

The big man spun around, but Selena had hidden from view. He stumbled to his feet and reached for the rail to pull himself up into the plane, but the stairs were closing out of his reach as the jet taxied down the tarmac. Fatim, his friend, was leaving without him. His face set, he pulled a lighter out of his pocket, opened it, and tossed it on the trail of jet fuel. He watched mesmerized as the flames licked and followed the narrow path they took.

The jet lifted off the tarmac and exploded in a ball of flames.

Another gunshot rang out.

~

Police cars with lights flashing poured down the airport road.

Sam screamed and sank to his knees, "Selena! No! God, she can't be dead."

Will jogged around the corner. "No, mate. She's not on the plane. I saw her roll off the bloke's shoulders when I shot him in the leg. She's here somewhere."

"Selena, where are you, honey? Answer me."

Sam ran into the shadows one way and Will the other.

Jonas burst out of the first car and followed Sam. "What's going on here?" Sam ignored him and kept looking for Selena. The detective grabbed Sam's arm, "I asked you a question."

"Selena's here somewhere and probably hurt. Get out of my way."

Jonas gestured to a uniformed officer behind him. "We're looking for a female approximately thirty, possibly hurt. Notify the others and get some fire equipment out here."

Sam hurried toward the side of the older hangar.

Selena sat on the tailgate of the rental truck. "I thought this could be your rental," she whispered. "What took you so long?"

Chapter Thirty

Selena snuggled next to Sam on Montaire's private jet and took a deep breath. Toby was sound asleep on the sofa in the back of the cabin, and Will had walked forward to visit with the pilot. She was glad they'd chosen to fly back to Kansas with them instead of on a commercial flight.

She was tired, but sleep wouldn't come. The excitement was finally over with the time spent away from home eventful. Base didn't need to die like he did, but he no longer made a blot on the integrity of the principality. The box that he had sent the ransom note in belonged with the rest of Montaire's history, so with the woodworker's family's permission, it would go in the museum at the manor.

She didn't know why Ahmed shot himself after blowing up the plane, but it guaranteed other women like her would be safe from the sheik's grasp—at least through his son.

Michael moved the Townsend family from the cabin earlier that morning. He called when they were there and whined that Laura beat him, shooting baskets. A smile crossed her face when she remembered the girl crowing about her victory in the background. She and her puzzle box were safe at home with Angel. Michael would help in her recovery, and the Townsends would be good for him.

Selena was ready to be home and back to what she did best—research.

Sam's eyes narrowed on her lips, and he kissed her softly. "I thought I'd lost you," he whispered.

"You didn't. I thought you were asleep."

"No," he said. "Just thinking. There was something I planned to ask you after the wedding in a nice, romantic spot with the stars twinkling above, and no one else around. We almost had our time in the gazebo, then shots pinged around us. Then the sheik's son tried to run away with you... All I can say is you make life interesting."

Selena smiled. "Thanks, I think."

"It's useless to plan anything around you. I'll never be bored." He trailed a finger on her cheek. "You're pretty and smart and love the people I love. And you love the way I drive."

"I wouldn't go that far." She rolled her eyes at him.

He grinned, then the look in his eyes turned intense.

Selena's hands got clammy. "What were you going to ask me, Sam?"

He pulled a little box from his pocket and held it out for her. His brown eyes met her green ones.

She basked in the love she could see there, and her hands shook as she pushed the lid back. Two rubies set beside a single diamond solitaire that winked at her in the light.

Sam slid the ring on her finger. "I love you, Selena. Will you marry me?"

She stared at the ring, then said solemnly, "Only if you take driving lessons or let me drive. Will said you scared him today. Cars aren't toys, you know."

He grinned and took her in his arms.

Chapter
Thirty-One

*D*ear Journal: Today I married the man of my
dreams at our cabin in the woods under an
arbor decorated with red roses. Miss Essie
picked them out. A soft breeze ruffled my hair. The soft
white dress with its sweetheart neckline and wide lace
shoulder straps was perfect for an outdoors wedding in
Kansas. It flowed to my strappy silver sandals and
shimmered in the morning sunlight as Uncle David
walked me down the aisle. All I could see was Sam
waiting for me with tears glistening in his eyes. He
looked so handsome in his tux.

To have and to hold...

Now, I know what cherished means.

When the pastor pronounced us husband and wife,
and after Sam kissed me, I looked out into the faces of
friends and those we love and realized we have a
wonderful family—Uncle David, Matt and Haylie and
the baby to come, Aunt Essie, Michael and Angel, Laura,
and Pops, Will, and Toby. Dex made a fine ring bearer.

The day was perfect.

We'll renew our vows in Montaire. The people love
to celebrate, and all want to be part of the Contessa's

wedding. I will also be in on the decision to select a new council member. Maybe a woman this time? I know there will be lots of research on the candidates...

I wonder if Sam's realizes yet that today he became a count...

Did you read The Contessa's Necklace, book 1?

Linda Siebold, a life-long Kansan, writes Romantic Suspense. Her first published book The Contessa's Necklace was published in November, 2018.

Made in the USA
Lexington, KY
14 September 2019